LANDSLIDE

Hilton Jones

To Gill

Happy reading.

[signature]

ISBN: 9798390681473

ii

Prologue

The windscreen wipers barely coped with the rain lashing down from the pitch-black sky. Reflections of his headlights in the curtain of rain ahead made the driver's progress difficult by reducing the range of his vision to that of a November fog.

'God, I hate this weather!'

That thought had been uppermost in his mind ever since he'd left Rosslare for the crossing to Fishguard and had been repeated aloud many times as the weather had deteriorated through the climb into the mountains.

Sticking to the motorways - M4 to Bristol, M5 to Birmingham, M6 to Manchester - would have been far easier, particularly as the suggestion of one of his mates took him on to narrow roads with not even white lines to keep him on the straight and narrow - or, in his case, the winding and narrow. There were no police patrols, though, out here in the wilds. At least that was a bonus.

The rain had been bad enough at sea level, but as he drove away from the coast and climbed into the mountains, words like 'torrential' and 'blinding' passed through his mind as the storm intensified.

He considered stopping to let it pass, but in the darkness, no lay-by offered itself - none that he could make out, anyway - just a few passing places which were far too short to accommodate his articulated vehicle, so he pressed on.

Only a hundred more miles to Manchester, give or take.

A finger-post stood at a junction. He could just about make out 'Llanynder' as the route to follow.

'What's that in English?' he muttered. 'They all look the same to me.'

Had it been a fine summer's day, he would have been marvelling at the terrific views from the crest of Mynydd Mawr before beginning the descent to the lowlands of the Severn Valley beyond. Alongside him, a ravine, at the bottom of which ran the River Gwennan, a moody river which, after all this rain, would be flouncing and bouncing, excited in a tearing rush to meet the Severn some miles to the east.

But this driver and his lorry would not reach that confluence. Suddenly, the road heaved and bucked beneath him as the side of the mountain, weakened by the vast amount of water that had fallen upon it in the previous weeks, slipped away, depositing trees, rocks, tarmac and lorry into the valley below. The driver was flung about his cab, gripping the steering wheel in the vain hope of steering out of trouble, as the vehicle rolled and bounced into the blackness until his head hit the side window and a permanent blackness ended his life.

His passengers, locked in the container at the rear, were oblivious to what was happening outside. They had heard the driving rain on the sides of the vehicle and they had realised that they were climbing - some ears had popped as the altitude increased and they sensed the downward changing of gears as their driver picked his way into the mountains but that was all they knew. They were thousands of miles from home, in a foreign country which they had, up to now, regarded as a refuge.

Bodies were flung violently against the metal sides. Heavy boxes, stacked at the rear of the container to hide the living cargo up front from the prying eyes of Border Force, bounced about,

2

causing more injuries, The smell of blood from their injuries was overpowered by the stench from the makeshift toilet - an oil-drum in the corner - as it was overturned.

A massive rock rolled down the mountain and bounced on the top of the container, overtaking it and tearing a hole in the corner, as it came to rest ahead of the falling lorry, halting the vehicle's fall and allowing yet more of the avalanche of the descending landscape above to coat the container with a deep layer of earth, bushes and bracken. The Gwennan was already diverting itself around the growing mound of earth. Cries and screams went unheard in the hell of the storm; the maelstrom of noise had been augmented by the clanging of the metal container as it rolled down the mountainside.

There were twenty fearful souls, some of which had already passed into the next world, in the melee, enclosed in a metal prison - a prison which had held the promise of freedom - a prison from which there was no escape - doomed to a slow, miserable death in the cold, damp gloom of a wild Welsh mountainside.

One

I looked across the rim of my pint glass at the young man opposite, then tilted it in a toast.

'Cheers and welcome back,' I said

That afternoon, I had been doing the rounds of the school, making sure that all was locked up safely at the end of the day, when I exited through the front door to find a young man, smiling and holding out a hand for a friendly hand-shake.

'Hello again, Mr Evans,'

Momentarily at a loss, my brain scanned through all the faces that had passed through this door in the years I had been caretaker at the Primary School, hundreds of young faces; but the way he said my name, his neat appearance and the honest eyes rang bells from thirty years ago.

'David?' I asked. 'David Pearce?'

'Right first time,' he laughed. 'You've got a good memory, Mr Evans.'

We shook hands enthusiastically, glad to see each other again, though the last time I had seen him, he had been eleven years old. Even back then, he was older than his years; responsible, resourceful, caring. His firm hand-shake told me that nothing had changed.

'I was passing through Llanynder, meeting a client further up the mountain, and I just had to call to see you.'

'I'm glad you did, David.'

The initial reunion over, we acknowledged that we both had work to do, so we agreed to meet later at *The Horseshoe* to catch up on our recent histories.

The fire burned brightly in the snug of *The Horseshoe* that evening, reflecting off the polished brassware in the nooks and crannies around the room as David and I took our pints across to the well-worn but comfortable armchairs before the fire.

David returned my toast.

'Cheers,' he said. 'It's great to be back.'

'Well,' I began, 'You've seen me at work. Still at the school. But it's always interesting because you get new staff, new children, new ideas every year, so you could say nothing changes, but at the same time, nothing stays the same. And what's been happening with you?'

David took a long sip of his pint before he told me that he had gone to Law School and was now a solicitor with none other than Rhodri, Jacson and Davies, the firm I had dealt with so many years ago.

'Is Miss Lansley still there?' I asked. 'Brenda Lansley' I added, in case further identification were needed.

'She's Mrs West now. Yes, she's still there, keeping everything in order. We couldn't manage without her.'

My mind went back thirty years, to a day when Brenda and I had felt so close. I recalled her tear-stained face looking up at me, the tear tracks illuminated by the glow from the flames of Frondeg. We had been close enough to be lovers, but not close enough to make it a permanent arrangement. Perhaps it was the emotion of the moment, having escaped so narrowly from a dangerous situation, which threw us together, but in the passage of time, we grew apart and had not seen each other for some time

Added to which, Bethan Fox and I had spent time together, consoling each other. Two bereaved souls, each hurting from the loss of a friend which had left a sudden gap in their lives. I had lost Cathy, she had lost her policeman husband, Lawrence, both violently. It was inevitable that we would grow together, and we eventually married twenty-five years ago.

I related all this to David, who listened, and commented, sympathetically.

'Didn't I hear that you were in Manchester? How did that come about?' I asked.

'After Law School I worked with a Liverpool firm, Woodroffe and Blaze, at their Manchester office,' he said. 'Criminal law. I spent a lot of time in court. Gang warfare in the North West produced a lot of work as the police made arrest after arrest every week. Shootings were a regular occurrence in the early days; nowadays, the knife seems to be the weapon of choice. I moved up the firm as I gained experience though I'm still too young to be a partner in such a big company.'

'So how does a successful criminal lawyer from Manchester suddenly pop up at a quiet backwater like Pont Owain? I haven't heard of a crime wave sweeping the valley,' I asked with a smile.

'Two things happened at the same time which put thoughts into my head. My parents are in their eighties and not in particularly good health. I've been so involved with my work in Manchester that I've spent too little time with them, just fleeting visits a couple of times a year. They need me now, so I've come home to roost, you might say.'

'And what was the other thing?' I asked, nodding approval at the first.

' A partnership at Rhodri, Jacson and Davies was advertised, as Mr Day finally decided to retire. He felt it was time he went. He was ninety last week, you know. Still as sharp as ever, a wonderful man.'

'Yes. I met him briefly, many years ago.'

'So,' David went on, 'those two things helped me make up my

6

mind to come home. I re-trained in Family Law. It's so different from dealing with criminals, but very rewarding, nevertheless.'

We talked on into the evening.

David had played Rugby League as a student in Lancashire, but a shoulder injury had curtailed this activity and he had taken up hill walking to maintain his fitness. He looked forward to walking in Wales once more - up to now he had walked the Peak District, with occasional visits to the Lake District from his Derbyshire home.

He had also taken up hill walking for the solace it brought him following the tragic death of his young wife. Sallie was just twenty-five when she was gunned down in a drive-by shooting in Manchester. Whether this was a revenge attack following a successful prosecution or just collateral damage in a gang war and therefore classified as 'accidental' was never proved, but I suspected that it was another factor in David's decision to return to Wales. The 'unlawfully killed' verdict was cold comfort to the young solicitor.

David went to the bar to replenish our drinks and came back with a cup of coffee for himself and a pint for me, a thoughtful look on his face.

'You look serious,' I said. 'I didn't think that carrying a couple of drinks across the stone floor should have taken that much concentration.'

'Yes,' he said. 'A face from the past. At the public bar. What's he doing down here, I wonder?'

'Someone local?' I asked, intrigued that David looked so serious, almost worried, about the newcomer.

'No. Manchester. I'm sure he was a witness in a case I dealt with a few years ago. Some faces you don't forget and not everybody has a red rose tattoo on the back of his hand. Very interesting. He was deep in conversation with Gareth behind the bar. Seemed to be quizzing him. What about, I wonder?'

7

He stood up and looked out on to the car park. Apart from his black Mercedes and Gareth's bicycle leaning against a tree, the only other transport out there was a BMW, and he discreetly made a note of its number in his diary.

'Nothing to do with me, really,' he said 'But my suspicious mind can't help wondering what he's doing this far from Manchester. His mate didn't look too savoury, either. I just hope he didn't recognise me.'

'Would that be important?' I asked. 'You're a long way from Manchester here.'

'I know,' he replied, and went on to relate to me his long-held suspicion about his wife's death, as he was convinced that she had been the intended target in the shooting. 'We're dealing with determined people, and I had successfully prosecuted his boss just a few days before the shooting. Twenty years, he got, though he'll only serve ten. I'm sure the message went out to his henchmen to do something by way of revenge.'

'Do you think he might have traced you down here? This is mid-Wales, you know. And it's a long time since it happened.'

'I'm not sure. It could be a coincidence and I'd be worrying over nothing. But it's as well to be on my guard. These people have long memories, you know.'

The snug door opened and a head looked in.

'Sorry, wrong door,' it said and went away.

David looked again through the window as we heard the engine of the BMW rev up as it left the car park.

'Let's have a word with Gareth,' David said.

Gareth was polishing tables and washing glasses after his customers had left. Only David and I remained, so we went around to the public bar to find him.

He had taken over *The Horseshoe* from his father, Gordon, who had spent a lifetime behind that bar and Gareth had been brought up in the knowledge that one day it would be his. He therefore kept up his father's high standard of presentation and cleanliness. Gordon still lived in partial retirement in the upstairs flat at the pub, while Gareth had a cottage just a short cycle-ride away.

'You are David , aren't you?' Gareth asked as we approached.

'I am,' David replied, with a smile. 'Nice to see you again, Gareth. It's been a long time since we were at Llanynder school together.'

'That's true. You were the clever one who went off to university; I stayed at home and haven't moved since.'

'You run a very nice pub, though. It's a valuable part of the community. You can be proud of what you've done here.'

'Well, thanks. Do you know, I wasn't sure it was you when you came in and I didn't have chance to ask because there were other customers waiting to be served. You haven't changed much. Where have you been all this time?'

'Manchester, mostly, but I'm working in Pont Owain, now. I'm with Rhodri, Jacson and Davies.'

'Oh, a solicitor then. Useful man to know. It must be a coincidence, but the last customer was from Manchester. Not the type to get into an argument with, I wouldn't have thought.'

'He seemed to be chatty, though, when I came up to the bar.'

'Yes. Asked some strange questions, though. Do we get many lorries on this road? Is this the way to South Wales? How far is it to the sea? Obviously, no sense of geography.'

'What did you tell him?'

'Well, this isn't a through road to anywhere. As Mr Evans will tell you, David, we used to have the occasional artic through, in the middle of the night mostly, but since the landslide up at Mynydd Mawr there's been nothing, of course. It'll be years before they replace the road up there.'

'Yes, very odd questions, as you said.'

David seemed satisfied with that and we said our farewells.

9

'Let me give you a lift to your cottage,' David said as we left. It was a welcome suggestion. The walk home would have been no problem, but David seemed keen to talk and I was interested to listen, so I accepted.

As he drove, he said 'When I said that I was seeing a client further up the mountain, it was actually a site meeting at the landslide that happened a few weeks ago. I was meeting my client and the local councillor with a surveyor from the Highways Department of the County Council on site to talk about compensation and the way forward. The landslide has cut his farm in two, with no access between the two halves as the road has gone. His insurance company was treating it as an act of God; he's calling it an act of the Devil, As Gareth said, it's likely to be years before the road is re-instated. The whole side of the mountain just moved down. The Gwennan has diverted itself around the debris so there has, fortunately, been no flooding. It was massive. The only reason it didn't make the TV news is that it's so isolated up here it's not considered important. No houses were demolished; no one was killed; not newsworthy at all. So, why would that guy from Manchester be asking questions about lorries and routes to the sea? Something to think about over your bedtime drink.'

We pulled up outside my cottage by the school.

'I'll give you a ring when I've given it some thought,' he said as I got out of the car. For my part, I was a little puzzled as to his sudden interest in the BMW driver. We exchanged phone numbers and he drove on home.

I watched the tail lights disappear down the road to Pont Owain. I had something to think about. Was there anything in David's supposition? Had he really come back to hide from whatever had happened in Manchester? Perhaps his concern for his parents was just coincidental to the threat of retribution.

Two

I often sat in my little cottage, enjoying the view down to the River Severn across the fields. The first field was the school sports field, which was maintained by the county council. Not my problem. The gardens between the field and the school building were another matter; they were the source of the vegetables for the school dining room. The children enjoyed the results of my labours; for instance, on the days it was served at lunch, the rhubarb crumble was extremely popular. They had watched the rhubarb grow through the previous weeks from a dead looking crown in March to reach its full glory of sturdy stems in June. These were country kids, used to the ways of nature. Many of them lived on farms, or their parents worked on farms, so they were knowledgeable about sowing and growing, about birth, death and everything in between.

Some of them were playing at the riverside, and they had discovered a plastic bottle on the bank, left behind by the receding water following the recent storms. Inside, they could see paper with writing on it, strange writing, which they described as 'funny writing'.

Where had it come from? The label on the bottle was little help, extolling the dull orange liquid which had been within as 'The Best in Ireland' in a mediaeval font, unfamiliar to young eyes.

Admittedly, what they could see of the rolled-up paper inside would certainly look odd to children. I could imagine their conversation. 'Let's go and ask Mr. Evans. He's been abroad. Perhaps he can understand it.'

Barely able to contain their excitement, they ran up the field with their find. 'We think it's a treasure map! Can you get it out for us, please?' they asked.

I examined the bottle. Fortunately, nothing had been damaged as they had been unable to unscrew the cap to extricate the paper. Indeed, with my hand that had left two fingers in the Falklands in 1982, it took some effort for me to gain entry and carefully pull out the loosely rolled-up piece of paper. The writing on it really did look strange, even to my eyes, and I put it aside to research its language and maybe even translate it later. It may be a joke or perhaps something serious. The writing had some form about it, not just idle scribbling; the chance that it was serious grew in my mind. At least, it was not a treasure map; the children were disappointed and went back to playing on the river bank.

According to the label, the bottle had contained an orange drink, made by McFadden's of Dublin. The label had been printed in a Gaelic font to give the locally-made orange juice some identity, some authenticity. How had an Irish bottle found its way to mid-Wales? We have tourists in Wales - hundreds, probably thousands of back packers and hikers walking the hills and valleys - anyone could have brought it. And what about the foreign writing on the paper? Again, the possibilities were endless. In the face of these odds, I gave up on supposition and turned on my computer to try to identify the writing. It did not take long for me to establish that the language was Korean, but finding an interpreter might take a little longer. The source of the note intrigued me, but not to the extent that I would drop everything in its favour, though the conundrum of what a Korean would be doing in Wales with a bottle of Irish orange juice did raise my interest more than a notch.

However, try as I might, I could not shake the puzzle out of my mind, and after a restless night, during which Koreans, Irishmen and Welshmen appeared and disappeared through my dreams, I rose early and decided to try to trace the source of the message. The bottle had come out of the river, so a walk upstream may lead to a clue as to its origin.

Thirty years ago, when Bethan had been left alone following Lawrence's untimely death, she had continued to live at the police house, but there were too many memories for her to stay there, and she moved into my cottage. Added to which, she was nervous about being left alone, recalling the night that Brenda had sat with her following Lawrence's death. She felt safe with me and it was not very long before we tied the knot.

Following my restless night, I breakfasted with Bethan - my usual porridge followed by toast and marmalade - and told her what I had planned to do.

'You'll be taking Jess with you, then?' she asked, knowing the answer would be in the affirmative.

Jess was a rescue dog who returned our kindness in taking her in with loyalty, obedience and companionship. A black and white Collie, she was a carbon copy of Nell, my first dog, who had died so violently thirty years ago, an event that I could never forget. Like Nell, Jess was our self-appointed guard dog; she always stayed with Bethan when I was busy, but this morning, I felt that she might benefit from a long walk.

'I'd like to take her,' I replied, though I sensed that Bethan would have preferred Jess to stay at home with her. 'Why don't you come with us? It's a long time since we walked the river bank together.'

Bethan brightened at the idea. She had been a keep fit fanatic at one time, but running around the lanes and hills held too many threats in her mind and her blonde pony-tail and her pink tracksuit ceased to be seen out and about. However, the thought of coming out with me felt safe, with the added comfort of Jess for company.

13

The morning sun warmed the breeze on our faces as we set off from the cottage, following the Severn, and a mile upstream we reached the confluence with the Gwennan. Which to follow? We decided that the Gwennan would be the shorter and after a stop for refreshment in Pont Owain, we pressed on until we came to the site of the landslide. We had heard talk about the extent of the earth movement, but we were completely amazed by what we saw as we approached.

The whole side of the mountain had moved down. Broken soil five hundred feet up to our right and the two-hundred-yard base of the disturbed earth down below were evidence of the extent of the landslide. Trees and rocks showed amongst the debris, mingled with lumps of tarmac here and there, the remains of the road that passed through here.

At the bottom, the Gwennan, as David had said, had diverted itself around the heap of soil, as always, in its rush to join the Severn lower down the valley. Jess ran about, investigating the broken ground. She had picked up a scent which held her interest and she started digging, her forepaws scrabbling at the soil.

'What has she found?' Bethan asked.

'Probably an animal caught in the landslide,' I replied and called to Jess to leave it. 'It's been dead for a week. She'll only want to roll in it afterwards, and we'll have to live with the rotten smell for days,' I explained, and we moved off to follow the Gwennan's new route around the changed landscape, joined, reluctantly, by Jess.

Half a mile farther on we encountered a grating in the river which was blocked with branches and leaves brought down by the rushing waters.

'That's the end of our search, then,' I said. The bottle must have come down the Severn, not the Gwennan. We haven't seen anywhere where anyone had camped for the night, so we must have chosen the wrong river to follow. Perhaps we can do the

Severn on another day. Or perhaps we've got it wrong and we've been on a wild goose chase anyway.'

Needing a respite from walking, Bethan and I sat on a grassy bank. She opened the sandwiches we had brought while I poured hot coffee from a flask.

'But haven't we had a good day out together, though?' she said. She was looking more relaxed than I had seen her for weeks. Younger, too. Her blue eyes sparkled again. Her pony-tail was still as blonde as ever, if you ignore the odd streak of grey, which told of her tragic experiences years ago. I pulled her to me, with an arm around her shoulders. We shared a kiss and Jess shared the moment by coming to sit on our feet.

Walking home together was a pleasure. The end of an almost perfect day. If we had found the source of the bottle it would have been perfect.

Three

After work next day, my mind returned to the note that the children had found. Staring at it was not going to improve my understanding, but it was all I could do at this stage, and I thought that a phone call to David might relieve my frustration. Perhaps he was more computer-savvy than I was and could suggest how to get a translation of it.

He answered his mobile by the second ring and after the pleasantries I explained my predicament.

'And you think it's in Korean?' he asked. 'That's difficult. You would have a job to translate it in Google.' He thought for a moment. 'There's a Korean restaurant in Shrewsbury, I think it's called *The House of Kimchi*. Look it up. They may be able to help.'

I thanked him and rang off. I would have to wait until the weekend to make a visit.

I sat in the lounge, staring once again at the note, as if a translation would eventually appear.

'Did David come up with anything useful?' Bethan asked as she whisked around with a duster.

'Yes, he suggested a Korean restaurant in Shrewsbury may be able to help.'

'So when are you going?' she asked. She knows me so well.

'I can't go until the weekend. How would you like to go to the cinema? We haven't been for a long time. Then we could go to this restaurant afterwards.'

She gave the idea her enthusiastic approval. We always enjoyed a day out together, whether it was walking the river bank or even the odd day trawling round shops, though neither of us relished spending much time in town.

On Saturday afternoon, we found the film to be quite entertaining and I managed not to fall asleep for once, to Bethan's great amusement. I have been known to sleep through some of the most exciting films, but this one had held my attention.

We found *The House of Kimchi* on the south side of Shrewsbury, close to the cinema. The outside looked welcoming, with tastefully draped curtains at the windows and bowls of flowers in the entrance.

A smiling waitress led us to our table and took our drinks order. We studied the menu, but as complete newcomers to Korean food, we had no idea what to order and settled for the advice of our waitress. This turned out to be excellent – at least we know what to order next time we're in a Korean restaurant.

Having paid, I asked our waitress whether she could help me with a translation.

She looked around; everyone was engaged in eating or conversation, or both.

'Yes, but I must be quick,' she said, glancing at her boss, then taking the paper from me, smoothing it out.

She read it through quickly and her hand went to her mouth, her eyes filled with tears, and she thrust it back to me.

'I can't tell you now. The boss is looking,' she said, and vanished through a beaded curtain into the kitchen, followed by her boss, a thick-set man who barked orders to the staff at every opportunity.

We stood, non-plussed. What had upset her so much? We waited for her to reappear. Raised voices came from the kitchen. The waitress returned, still visibly upset, carrying two plates of food and, having served the waiting diners, turned to us.

'I'm sorry, but I can't talk to you now.'

'What time do you finish work?' Bethan asked.

'Eleven o'clock tonight. I'm off tomorrow, though.'

'Can we meet you tomorrow?' I asked.

'Yes. How about on the Welsh Bridge. Ten o'clock. Look after the note. Don't lose it.'

'OK,' I said. But what's it all about? And what's your name? I'm Hugh and this is Bethan, by the way.'

'I'll tell you tomorrow. My name is Grace. I must go. My boss...'

She vanished again through the beaded curtain, wiping her streaming eyes with a table napkin.

Bethan and I left, mystified as to what the note contained and the tears it had generated. It would be a long wait until tomorrow.

Four

We rarely travel to Shrewsbury on consecutive days; once a month is enough, but this was exceptional. Grace's reaction had taken us by surprise; she had seemed positively upset by the note and we, obviously, couldn't know why. We wondered what we would find out when we met on Sunday morning.

It was, fortunately, a sunny day when we met Grace on the Welsh Bridge and we found a riverside café where we could talk.

Grace seemed subdued; she was clearly worried about the contents of the note, but she bravely took it from me. She read it through again and once more the tears welled up. She finally composed herself and read the note to us.

'*Dear Father*,' she read.

'*This is the last you will hear from me. I am sorry that the money you paid for me and Eun-jung to come to Europe was wasted.*

We left home on Buddha's Birthday and we have now reached UK, but we are trapped with the others in a container. Our lorry crashed and nobody knows we are here. Over the last week, everyone has died from injuries and lack of water. My little sister was among the first to die and I will be the last.

Goodbye and thank you for trying to help us to a better life.

From your grateful son Min-jun.'

Grace finished by saying that it was addressed to Mr Geldong at Postal code 40326.

By the time she had finished, not only was Grace in tears, so was Bethan. I must confess to a lump in my throat as well.

'That's so sad,' said Bethan 'How can you explain it?'

Grace took a moment to dry her eyes and take a sip of the coffee.

'I agree. It's very sad. It sounds as though they are people who have left Korea and hope to settle here. Like my parents did.'

'They were immigrants?' I asked.

'Yes, but not illegal. They were refugees.'

'What's the difference? Bethan wanted to know.

'North Korea calls people who leave, defectors. If they go north to China, the Chinese send most of them back and they are imprisoned for disloyalty. They could even be executed for 'treason to the nation'. If they go to South Korea, they are welcomed by the government with financial grants and free education at first, but they are often treated as second-class citizens by the South Koreans, so
life is still difficult for them. But if they then decide to come to Europe, they cannot claim to be escaping persecution because they are now coming from South Korea. The only way is to try the illegal route. London has the largest population of Koreans in Europe, and the whole world knows you have democracy here, something that's missing in their homeland, so this is the destination of choice. As my parents came direct from North Korea they were classed as refugees. I was born here.'

'That explains your English accent,' I said.

'Yes, but I can speak and read Korean as well.'

'Of course. And it's so kind of you to come out and meet us today, we couldn't have blamed you if you hadn't turned up once you knew what this note contained.'

'I couldn't do that. Can I ask how you got the note?'

'I live near the Severn, up in mid-Wales and it came down the river in a bottle. Some children found it and brought it to me because the writing they could see inside looked funny, as they called it. They thought it might be a treasure map!'

'I wish it had been. But it seems absolutely genuine.'

'Do you think it was written recently?' Bethan asked.

.Grace looked at the note again.

'He mentions Buddha's birthday. That would have been in May.'

I added that the label on the bottle was not faded in any way, it was not a year old, so it must have been put into the river recently.'

Grace continued, 'It looks as though...' she paused to glance at the note '...Min-jun wanted to let his father know of his fate. But why would he put it in the river? Have there been any lorry crashes that you know of?'

'None at all,' I said, 'But he says they have died over the last week. Surely someone would have noticed a crashed lorry in that time. Or the owners would be looking for it. If it had gone off the road, perhaps it could be hidden by trees. It could hardly be buried.'

These possibilities whirled around in my head. Could it be buried? Could someone be looking for a lorry? Surely not. That's all conjecture. Coincidence. I couldn't speak because I didn't know where to start. They would think I was off my head to suggest what I was thinking. But it was the only solution in my fuddled brain. Clear as crystal. The BMW driver at *The Horseshoe* the other night. A massive landslide up the valley. Was it big enough to bury a lorry? Had Jess found a clue? My Army training from long ago kicked in and the way forward was clear. There was only one way to find out.

'I've got an idea. We'll have to go up the valley to check. Have you any plans for today or would you like to come with us? I'll bring you back later,'

'I've nothing planned. Of course I'll come with you.'

'What have you thought of? asked Bethan.

21

'I'll tell you in the car. Come on.'

As I drove out of Shrewsbury, I took the opportunity to tell them what I had thought. It still sounded logical, logical and far-fetched at the same time. At least they went along with the idea without any deprecating comments.

We called at my cottage, where I put on my hiking boots and collected a torch and a spade. Bethan changed her town shoes for a pair of hiking boots and lent Grace a pair of wellingtons. Jess was not to be left out. The sight of us putting on our boots meant only one thing - a walk, though she was more than a little puzzled to see us getting into the car. This was going to be quicker than walking alongside the Gwennan up to the site of the landslide.

We drove until we ran out of tarmac, where bright orange plastic barriers blocked the way to anyone foolish enough to want to go further into the gaping slash in the landscape.

Taking our tools, we scrambled down into the ravine, passing upended trees, rocks that had never seen the light of day until now, chunks of tarmac, clumps of bracken from higher up the mountain, gorse and heather, also relocated from higher up. An apocalyptic scene.

Jess thought this was great fun and ran ahead, nose close to the ground. I've often wondered about a dog's view of the world. A kaleidoscope of smells and scents to be investigated. The nose as accurate as radar, guiding them to their next adventure. But instead of casting around, she had now homed in on an interesting scent, at the same spot that had been so interesting on our last visit.

We paused in our scrambling and assessed the situation. The broken soil and trees at unnatural angles created a bizarre scene. Grace was amazed at the sight of the devastation and was trembling with anticipation of what we might find if my supposition was correct.

Jess moved on, having drawn a blank at her first site and was casting around on a fresh hunt. A pile of gorse bushes and heather caught my attention. I still felt, like the others, that the burying idea was too far-fetched, but I pushed aside the overhanging greenery ahead of me. White metal protruded through the soil. I used my spade to investigate further. My blood ran cold when, after very little digging, I could see that this was, indeed, a corner at the front end of what could only be a shipping container. Buried in soil and camouflaged by the gorse and heather, it was completely hidden from view, even from us as we stood nearby. Bethan and Grace clutched each other's hands, dreading the thought of whatever was to come.

A small part of the top corner of the container had been torn as it rolled and bounced down the mountain, leaving a small hole which was big enough to put an arm through but too small to climb through. By now, I was convinced that this was the lorry we were looking for. I asked Bethan to hand me the torch, though I was not ready to see what would be illuminated through the hole.

I knelt next to the hole and pushed Jess away from investigating a new smell. As I bent closer, the smell hit me. My torch highlighted parts of the horrific scene as I moved the beam from side to side. The tangle of bodies within had clearly been dead for some time, with the inevitable odour of death. Emaciated bodies lay at grotesque angles, with savage injuries from the heavy boxes which must have been flung about as the lorry fell into the valley. Plastic bottles and sandwich wrappings littered the dark corners of the container. An oil drum on its side suggested that their makeshift toilet had been upended, adding to the smell. Nearest to the hole I could make out a young man with a little girl, no more than eight years old, in his arms. Min-jun had ensured that his little sister was accompanied to whatever resting place his religion required.

I told Bethan and Grace what I had seen and gave them the choice of whether they would like to look inside. They declined. My description had been gruesome enough, even though I had kept

23

details to a minimum.

'We'll have to tell the police,' I said, 'but there's no mobile signal up here. We'll ring from home on the landline.'

There was nothing more we could do at the site. No way could I dig a lorry out single-handed. We returned to the car.

Bethan and Grace were naturally subdued on the way home.

Bethan put her thoughts into words.

'It's so sad. They left Korea to get away from the hardships. They went through God knows what hardships to travel halfway around the world to get here, just to end like this. Why is the world so unfair?'

There was no answer any of us could give.

Five

Detective Inspector Maldwyn Humphreys listened patiently as I told him the background to my discovery.

'This was the second time you had been up to the site?' he asked.

'Yes. The first time, my wife and I went on foot, looking for somewhere that someone have may have camped for the bottle to have ended up in the river. As we saw nothing to suit that description, we assumed it had come down the Severn, and that would have been a much longer search. We probably wouldn't have bothered. Do you realise, if the note had been in English, we would have thought it was a hoax; somebody larking about. It was only Grace's reaction and her knowledge of immigrants, that convinced us that it was serious and led us to look for a lorry up at Mynydd Mawr.'

'Well, I'm glad you did. Though my boys didn't care for being called out on a Sunday evening.'

'Will there be someone up there all night?'

'Yes. We have to secure the site. I'll need you to come up with me in the morning to explain what you did up there, though I doubt there will be any clues external to the lorry as it's buried and out of view.'

'How will you dig it out?' I asked.

'We'll have to get an excavator up there as soon as we can. It's a massive job. Precarious, too. It will take an expert operator to work on the mountainside.' He was foreseeing the problems with some trepidation. A task of this complexity was outside the experience of most policemen.

'Getting it up there will also be a problem. These roads were only built for horse and cart, not the huge transporters we have these days.'

'What about a helicopter?' I asked. 'We used them in the Falklands years ago. Chinooks. Huge things. They can lift and carry massive weights. I'd say that was the only way you'll get a digger up there to do any good.'

'They'll be for military use only, I should think,' he said, still looking on the downside.

'There's no harm in asking,' I tried to lift his mood. 'It's a national problem, so I'm sure the government will help. It will be all over the papers when the news breaks. They will want to look good. They can't say 'no', can they?'

'I'll see what I can do,' he said, sounding a little more positive. We arranged for me to go up to the crash site after I had got the school running next morning; I would be there by 10am.

Now, as I had to return Grace to Shrewsbury, we hung up. Bethan had made some sandwiches and her always excellent Victoria sponge cake for us to sit down to tea with Grace before we left.

For her part, Grace was very subdued. I had brought her out here in tragic circumstances. Bethan and I had found it sad, but Grace felt very close to the victims in the lorry; even though she had been born in this country, they were her countrymen and women. And Min-jun and his sister, Eun-jung, entwined together in death, made it even more poignant. I drove her back to Shrewsbury and she made me promise to keep her informed about her compatriots in the lorry.

Later that evening, I rang David to give him the news of our discovery and to thank him for the tip about the Korean restaurant. He was, suddenly, extremely interested. How many bodies? Had I

26

seen the number plate? Any identifiable marks on the lorry? A name on the side? I stopped the machine-gun flow of questions by telling him that the lorry was still buried and would continue to be until tomorrow.

'Ring me as soon as you know something positive. Any identification. Incidentally, have you mentioned anything to the police about that guy at *The Horseshoe* who was asking about lorries the other night?'

'No,' I said. 'They didn't ask and I was perhaps a bit shell-shocked after my discovery so I didn't mention it. Why? Is it important?'

'It could be. I'd be interested to find out as much as I can about the lorry and what it was carrying. It's a long shot, but if Red Rose Man was interested in it, I'd like to see if there's any connection with Sallie's killers.'

He had clearly never got over his wife's death, though I failed to see how her shooting ten years ago would have anything to do with a recent lorry crash. His description of the gangs having long memories applied equally to himself.

I agreed to keep him informed when more details were available.

The flurry of police vehicles driving up the road to Mynydd Mawr on Sunday evening roused not a little interest in the village as they passed through and rumours were rife, even in the sparsely populated countryside.

As a result, when I arrived at the site on Monday morning, I had quite a walk past the parked cars of onlookers who had come to see what was going on. A murmur of interest came from the gathered spectators as I passed through the police cordon to greet DI Humphreys.

'Good morning, Inspector,' I tried to sound upbeat, hoping that he would have positive news,

'Good morning, Mr Evans. Good news!'

His response was positive. At last!

He explained that overnight the phones had been ringing in Whitehall. His Assistant Commissioner had contacted the Home Office, who had rung the Ministry of Defence who in turn had spoken to the RAF at Odiham in Hampshire, where the country's helicopters were based. This morning, he had received a call from Odiham, to say that they were dispatching a Flight Lieutenant and ground crew to assess the situation and co-ordinate the work plan. They would be here by mid-day and would be the ground contact with the helicopter when it arrived.

'So, the recovery is taking shape?' I commented.

'Yes,' he said. 'It's not a job I'm looking forward to. Usually, when I go to a murder scene, there's only one body to look at, and that's difficult enough. But if there are as many as you said in this one, it will be gruelling. But let's get on.' He led the way down the slope towards the lorry.

I showed him where I had parted the bracken and bushes and pointed out the hole in the lorry body. I handed him my torch to look into the hole. He took his time, shining the light at different angles to see as much of the interior as possible. His face was a shade paler when he turned to me.

'It's a terrible sight. I could make out at least ten bodies. Lots of boxes scattered about. We'll know more when we can get in, but there are no signs of life.'

He looked around the site and pointed out a field fifty yards away that had not been touched by the landslide.

'We will have to keep the spectators away from up there as we take the bodies out into the ambulances. We can also use that field for a landing site for the helicopter, should we need it. It the flattest field around here, so it should be ok.'

'So you'll take the bodies out of the lorry down here?' I asked.

'Yes, and take them up in body bags. It would be the final

indignity to leave them in the container while we lift it out. The ambulances can wait on that field and we'll put the barriers further down the road to keep the crowds at bay.'

'You're expecting crowds?'

'People have a macabre interest in someone else's misery. They'll be here, cameras at the ready, I guarantee it. Since the advent of mobile phones, everybody is a photographer. You've seen them on telly. They sell the footage of road crashes, fires, domestic rows to the TV companies. They film price tickets in the supermarkets, menus in restaurants. Kids in school play up in class and film the teacher's response. As I said, they'll be here.'

Unfortunately, he was right. Word had got round quickly and the road on both sides of the landslide was filling up even as DI Humphreys went up and instructed his men to move the barriers away from the field gate to keep the spectators, and reporters, further down the road.

It became obvious that DI Humphreys had been very efficient in organising his resources, as cars arrived carrying experts, a Council officer and paramedics. He gathered them into a marquee which his men had been busy erecting as he and I inspected the lorry. Tables and benches were laid out and a white-board was installed at the front, for him to explain the situation and his plan for dealing with it.

He deftly drew a sketch plan of the site, adding, ruefully, that he was no artist. It looked pretty good to me. I was grateful that he allowed me to sit in on the meeting, as I had been instrumental in finding it in the first place.

'Good morning, lady and gentlemen. Thank you all for arriving so promptly. My name is Detective Inspector Maldwyn Humphreys, and this is Mr Hugh Evans, who found the lorry and did some excellent work in establishing that it contains the remains of a group of, presumably, immigrants, all, unfortunately, deceased.'

He went on 'To start us off, perhaps you would all care to introduce yourselves.'

A well-built man spoke first.

'Will Croft. Logistics Manager of Diggahire Limited'

He sat next to a serious looking lady, brunette, in her thirties.

'Janet Wilshaw, Staffing Officer, County Council.

'I'm Jim Broadis, Medivent Limited. We provide medical cover at all kinds of events and we have a fleet of 15 ambulances, which I understand, will be necessary here,' said the third man, who had a bald head and a pleasant face. A smile was never far from his lips.

'Why aren't the NHS doing it?' Will Croft wanted to know.

'If there had been any survivors, the NHS would have dealt with them. The rest would be left to us. As it is regarded as a crime scene, the police are responsible for it and we are engaged to supply all facilities, including mortuaries.' Will was satisfied with Jim's explanation.

Maldwyn Humphreys carried on. 'Thank you for that. Now, we are awaiting the arrival of a Flight Lieutenant and ground crew from the RAF. They are travelling up from Hampshire and will be with us by mid-day.'

'What's the RAF got to do with this? It sounds serious,' Will Croft put in.

'It is serious. We're having to use a helicopter, so any plans we make may need to be changed in the light of any limitations the helicopter crew may put on us.'

He turned to the whiteboard to illustrate his explanation.

'In a nutshell, the outline plan will be to use the helicopter to lift an excavator into the crash site, which will then remove soil from the lorry. When we get access to the container, the medical team can remove the bodies to this field for removal to a mortuary. We will then need to remove the lorry body, probably by helicopter, and then remove the excavator, also by helicopter. Put this way, it sounds simple, but I am sure you realise that there will be problems all the way.'

Will Croft spoke first. 'An excavator will come from our Telford factory on a low-loader. It will take under two hours from when I ring to tell them which one to bring. I'll have to liaise with the RAF team over this. By its nature, the landslide will have produced loose soil and the ground will be unstable as a result, so we will have to do a lot of digging and soil removal before we can start to work on the lorry. It will be a long job before the medics can go in, how long it will take will depend on further examination of the site.'

Humphreys nodded. Jim Broadis raised a hand. 'Have you any indication of how many bodies we're talking about?'

'I'm afraid not at this stage. There is a small hole about nine or ten inches across at the front of the container. I looked through it with a torch and I counted about ten. There may well have been others out of the range of my torch.'

Jim continued, 'Mr Croft mentioned … '

'It's Will,' from Mr Croft.

'Thanks. Er, Will mentioned it would take time. Would a week be a fair estimate? I can arrange for an inflatable mortuary to be erected tomorrow if that will help.'

'Good thought, Jim. It's going on my list,' Maldwyn replied, and jotted a note in his notebook.

'I'd need to look at the site to see what we're dealing with, so I would say it will be at couple of days, may be more, before your team can get in, Jim,' Will Croft responded to Jim's question.

Janet Wilshaw spoke next. 'When you rang, you asked me about a team of men able to assist in carrying the bodies off the crash site and up to the ambulances on this field. This I can do, though it will be a case of asking for volunteers as some people may not like the idea of carrying bodies. Rest assured, we will do our best to accommodate your plans. When you know how many you need and when you will need them and for how long, please ring me. I'll be setting the wheels in motion this afternoon.'

'I think we could do with two of Janet's men and one of \Jim's ambulances here right from the start tomorrow. We don't know what we are going to find, or when,' Maldwyn Humphreys said.

He seemed happy with what he had heard. He went on, 'Thank you, all, for your observations. Now you have seen the size and complexity of the operation, you realise that it will be a while before accurate timings can be decided. We don't want helpers standing around idle any more than you do, so I'll be in constant touch with you all. Now, if you'd like to put on the sensible footwear I asked you to bring, we can go down and look at the site.'

They were soon ready to make the descent.

Janet, it transpired, was a regular walker. She had done the Three Peaks twice and the Offa's Dyke all the way up the Welsh border, facts which she told us of when she emerged from her car in walking boots and waterproofs. Perhaps we men had been expecting her to be totally unprepared for rough terrain and the surprise on our faces prompted her explanation.

Down by the lorry, they could all see the enormity of the task ahead of us. Will was right about the unstable ground.

'At least, that rock below the lorry will help to stop it slipping when we start excavating.'

'How heavy is it, do you think?' Janet enquired.

'Five or six tons, at least,' he estimated.

Jim had spotted some paint on the corner of the rock.

'Do you think that made the hole in the corner of the container? The paint is the same,' he said.

True enough. The rock must have followed the lorry down the hill and its momentum had carried it over the lorry as it came to rest. It was fortuitous that, in striking the corner of the container and making a small hole, it had also allowed enough light in for

32

Min-jun to write his note and reach out to throw his bottle towards the river, which he would have heard rushing past just below. That information answered the questions in my mind about how the bottle had got into the river in the first place.

Maldwyn brought my mind back to the immediate problems.

'The lorry is lying on its side and the cab is at this end of the vehicle. Presumably the driver is still in it. So we'll have to dig him out, then move to the other end of the lorry to open the back. That will mean even more excavation over there.'

'That will be another job for the helicopter to lift the digger over,' I said, 'unless we cut the sides open at this end to gain access.'

'That sounds a better idea,' Will said,' There's a lot of soil to be shifted if we move over there; it will take days.'

Janet was concerned about the distance her team would be carrying the bodies.

'It's a steep climb up the bank, then almost a hundred yards down the road,' she said.

'Now we've seen the site, I think I'll only need to bring two ambulances. Your men can put the bodies into them to carry them down the road to the field,' Jim put in, adding 'There's plenty of room for a temporary mortuary on the field.'

'Excellent,' said Maldwyn, as he could see his experts beginning to gel as a team.

We made our way back up to the road in time to meet a newcomer – three newcomers, in fact. Maldwyn was pleased to find out that Flight Lieutenant Jack Gorrie and his two technicians, Flight Sergeant Tim Thompson and Sergeant Perry White had had no trouble finding us by road and had arrived early.

We all gathered in the marquee and introductions were made over welcome cups of coffee produced by one of Maldwyn's team.

He explained his plan to the RAF crew, who were in general agreement with the outline as we had heard before. Jack Gorrie and Will Croft were engaged in a conversation about the weight a Chinook could lift and which would be the appropriate digger to use. Janet and Jim were exchanging phone numbers to help the planning of removal of the bodies. Tim and Perry went outside with Maldwyn and familiarised themselves with the site, and I introduced myself to Maldwyn's constables, in case they were wondering how a civilian was involved.

When we reconvened later, the teams had established that we would only need the helicopter to lift the excavator in and out of the valley on dates which would be at least a couple of weeks apart. Jim and Janet's team would see to the removal of the bodies. The excavator could then clear the ground around the lorry to enable the vehicle to be cut up, though that would have to be agreed with the owners and their insurers, if we could find out who they were. There would be evidence of that in the cab, paperwork and such like, or Maldwyn could consult the police computer when we dug down to the number plate. Finally, the helicopter would return and the remains of the lorry could be lifted out, followed by the digger.

'Let's hope it all goes according to plan,' Maldwyn said, as we dispersed. 'We start tomorrow.'

It was encouraging, even exciting, when yesterday's plan swung into action.

The low-loader must have left base at a very early hour to arrive at Llanynder by eight a.m., closely followed by the arrival of the Chinook. Memories of the Falklands flooded back as the clatter of the rotors and the thunder of its engine vibrated through my body as it landed. At least, this time there were no soldiers with rifles running out from the back of it, some of them never to return. Had I been asked, I would have explained that I was drying my eyes because of the cold downdraught. Fortunately, I didn't have to explain, so no-one knew it would have been a lie.

By 9a.m. the low-loader, the Chinook and the first of the ambulances had been safely parked on the field and the crews briefed in the tent, where a generator provided electricity for the lights, the computers and charging the batteries of the cutters and angle grinders which our local blacksmith, Roddy Hughes, would need to carve a way into the container body.

The RAF boys had worked efficiently, and the digger had been safely lowered into the valley and had started clearing loose soil from the solid base to make a start on exposing the front end of the lorry.

By 10.30a.m. we found that the windscreen had survived the rolling fall; we could see the driver's body curled against the door, which was on the ground. Opening the passenger door to lift the driver out would have been difficult, as Jim pointed out that his curled-up body and the lack of space made it impossible. Instead, he suggested removing the windscreen altogether. This worked well. With the body on its way up the hill, Maldwyn took the opportunity to remove what papers he could find, as these would be invaluable for identification of the lorry and its driver. After a cursory glance through them, he asked me to take them up to his team, for them to extract all the useful information they contained. On the way up, I tried to memorise as much information as I could; the driver was Dan Brennan, according to his licence. This wasn't much, but on entering the marquee, I found it empty as both the constables were engaged on a mild crowd control issue on the roadside. I took out my mobile and photographed the pages on the clipboard.

Something for David, at last.

Six

'Rhodri, Jacson and Davies. How can I help you?'

I recognised the voice on the phone straight away.

'How are you, Brenda?' I asked, then added 'It's Hugh Evans, by the way.'

'I'm very well, thank you, Hugh. And yourself?'

'The same.'

We went through the pleasantries and she finally put me through to David.

'Information for you,' I told him, then related a summary of what had been going on, finishing with the details he had asked for, the lorry's registration number and the driver's name.

'Did you get your letter translated, by the way? You didn't tell me last night when you phoned.' he asked.

''I only gave you the bare bones. It was a short conversation,' I said. I didn't like to say that I could not get a word in as he was firing questions, almost not waiting for an answer.

'Yes. It was a useful tip, pointing me towards *The House of Kimchi*,' I went on. 'Their waitress, Grace, is from a Korean family but was born in this country. She was able to translate it easily; she also gave me some background on why Korean refugees travel to this country. It was all very sad to hear what life is like in North Korea, what hardships they have to face. Interesting, but sad.'

'So these were illegal immigrants in the lorry?' David asked.

'It seems so. I've photographs of some of the documents the driver was carrying. There's a delivery note for a consignment of 700 computers from an Irish company to a shop in Manchester...'

'That will be the cover for the trip,' David interrupted.

'...and it explains the boxes that I could see inside the container. I can imagine that those flying around as the lorry overturned would have caused some serious injuries.'

'Yes.'

'There's also a delivery note from a truck hire company in Manchester.'

'They might be worth a visit,' David said. He went on, 'If you could email those to me it would be very helpful.'

I sent them to him right away and returned to school that afternoon, my mind full of what had happened, full of questions. Why was David suddenly so interested? Why was the lorry on such a remote road? How had the immigrants got to Ireland? All questions that had no answers at the moment and, to be honest, had nothing to do with me, except for a natural desire to explain all the puzzles that life throws at us. And a feeling that I would like to find out more for Grace, who had been instrumental in setting the ball rolling.

School had finished early. The annual rounders match - Pupils versus Staff - had meant that everyone had been out on the field, so there was very little tidying up to do inside. There had been a short break in play to watch a Chinook as it clattered overhead on its way back to Odiham, its first commitment completed. The pupils went home victorious; the staff had retired exhausted to the staff room, leaving a clear run for the cleaners. We would be breaking up for the long summer holiday next day; I might be able to give more attention to the questions then.

Curiosity overcame me.

I delegated locking up duties to Mrs Potts's daughter, who had succeeded her mother in the post of Head Cleaner, and made my way up the road to Mynydd Mawr once again.

At the marquee, PC Derek Wynn brought me up to date with events.

The soil covering the front of the cab had been cleared and the windscreen removed to recover the driver's body. The late Dan Brennan had been carried up to the marquee and then taken by ambulance to the mortuary in Shrewsbury, a provisional forensic examination having concluded that the severe head injuries had been the most probable cause of his death.

DI Humphreys met me on the roadside.

'We're making good progress, Mr Evans,' he said. 'As it isn't practical to try to open up the rear of the vehicle, your blacksmith friend, Mr Hughes, is cutting away the sides of the container to give us access.'

He had obviously forgotten that it was at my suggestion that Roddy had been on standby for precisely this eventuality. Perhaps it would dawn on him later.

In the morning, Janet's and Jim's teams were joined by reinforcements.

Janet's carriers, hefty men who stretched their protective clothing to its maximum, and Jim's paramedics, whose overalls were more loose-fitting, were now waiting for the opportunity to start moving bodies from the container, having already dealt with the unfortunate Dan Brennan on the previous day. A large enough opening was finally made and the work to extract the bodies began. Thick rolls of hessian were placed over the sharp edges of the cut metal, to protect the workers and the immigrants as they were passed through the opening. The pair, who I thought could be Min-jun and his little sister were first out, having been carefully and lovingly separated from their final embrace. The poignancy of the moment was not wasted on the carriers; even these big men were seen to wipe their eyes, blow their noses or pull the peaks of their caps down to hide their emotions as the bodies of brother and sister emerged and were put into numbered body bags.

This harrowing scene was re-enacted several times through the day as more bodies were discovered and brought out. A small generator had been brought down to the site to provide light inside the container and a police photographer recorded each body found. In addition, a video was made of the whole tragic scene.

Meagre luggage was found, hardly qualifying for the title - just a small bundle wrapped in cloth and a small attaché case. Some sandwich wrappings from an Irish company floated in the mess lower down, together with about two dozen plastic orange juice bottles similar to the one which had started the whole discovery process off, on the river bank at Llanynder.

The lorry also carried a large cargo of computers, but nowhere near the seven hundred mentioned on the delivery note. These had been stacked at the rear of the container, presumably to hide the immigrants who were housed at the front, from the prying eyes of the port inspectors. From their final positions, it was clear that when the lorry rolled down the mountain, these heavy boxes had become missiles that had brought injury, and ultimately death, to the unfortunate passengers.

Seven

At home that evening, I related the day's happenings to Bethan. She hadn't really got over our experience on Sunday, when she and Grace had joined me at the crash site.

'Llanynder is only a little village. Disasters like this happen in other places, not here,' she said.

'Everyone says that when disaster strikes, but nowhere is exempt. Just think. The Twin Towers, Lockerbie, Aberfan, even Titanic. Nobody was expecting those, or many others you could mention,' I replied, adding 'Remember, we had a plane crash and all the explosions at Frondeg thirty years ago.'

'Of course. Poor Lawrence and Cathy. Both died horribly.' We both fell silent as we recalled our personal disasters, having lost our partners so viciously, cruelly, because of one man's wild ambitions.

Bethan broke the silence, going back to our original subject.

'Where was the lorry going to?' she asked.

'Manchester, as far as I could see on the paperwork.'

'Well we don't get many lorries up here, do we? Why was he coming this way?'

'Your guess is as good as mine, and mine would be that it's a quieter route and free of police patrols. Important when you're carrying an illegal cargo.'

The mention of the passengers brought tears to Bethan's eyes. 'Those poor people. They travelled across the world to get here. For what? To die on a mountainside. What a waste!'

My sweet Bethan. Always on the side of the underdog. Such a sentimental soul. There's not a vengeful bone in her body.

'Yes,' I agreed. 'A waste of their money to get here. A waste of all their efforts; the risk-taking; the hours, even days, of walking. And the people who they paid just sit back with not a care in the world as the money rolls in.'

'It seems trite to say 'Something ought to be done' but you feel so helpless in this situation. What can anyone do?'

We sat in silence as we mulled over the unfairness of the situation.

We settled down to watch television, though neither of us felt the need for entertainment. As I surfed through the channels, a news programme showed a banner for breaking news, announcing that twenty illegal immigrants and a lorry driver had died in a landslide in Wales. It went on to describe the situation at Mynydd Mawr, the size of the landslide, the diverted river, the helicopter and digger that had been used. The floodgates were open. We'd be flooded out with newspaper reporters and TV crews, all asking the same questions, all going away when the next newsworthy event took place elsewhere in the country.

The TV was interrupted by the ringing of the telephone. It was David.

'Sorry to bother you this late in the evening,' he began, 'but have you time for a chat?' he asked.

'Yes, of course,' I said, guessing that it could be about the lorry and its immigrant passengers.

'Don't ask me why, but I'm wondering if you might have the time to do a little running about for me.'

41

'I should think that 'Why?' would be the first question to come to mind. But go on, explain what you want me to do and then I'll decide.'

'I need to have some enquiries made,' he said.

'Don't you usually engage a private detective for that?' I asked.

'Normally I would, but I need someone completely anonymous, someone new to the area.'

'Which area are we talking about?' I asked, intrigued.

'Manchester, to start with, though there may be other places as well, depending on how the enquiries go. I thought, as you are now on school holidays, that you might have the time...' he left the conclusion in the air for me to fill in the blank. 'What do you think?'

'As long as it remains as 'enquiries', I could do something for you, I suppose.'

Of course I would do it, but there was no need to sound too enthusiastic. He seemed to have been dealing with some dangerous characters when he was up there in Manchester; if they were involved, I didn't really want to sound too keen to meet up with them. On the other hand, I felt a responsibility to the Koreans in the lorry. Grace's reaction made it personal; the letter from Min-jun – which still needed to be delivered to Mr Geldong - had brought me into his family, and as Bethan and I had just expressed our feelings, there was no way I was going to let matters rest with the police enquiries.

'Yes, I'll do it. What's the background?'

'I'd like to know more about this situation. I think a visit to Just Computers Ltd in Manchester is called for.'

'That's where the consignment was headed, wasn't it?'

'Yes. I've been looking through the lorry's paperwork that you sent me. You'll need to make up some kind of a story, but get an idea of what kind of business it is, where is it based, what kind of customers, you know what I mean.'

'OK so far,' I said. No fisticuffs in that. So far so good. 'What else do you want me to find out?'

'I'd like you to try to take a look at Denny Shaw Truck Hire. What kind of a company is it? This is just preliminary work and we don't want to raise any suspicions about our connection with the lorry. How do you feel about that?'

'It sounds OK. I'll keep my eyes and ears open. I'll go up tomorrow and fill you in when I get back.'

'Good man. But remember, Mr Evans, be careful.'

'I will,' I laughed. He was obviously recalling the difficulties I had encountered thirty years ago, when my cottage had been trashed and my Cathy, his teacher, had been killed because she knew too much.

We completed the call and rang off.

Eight

Early next morning, I set off alone, with only the car radio for company, for Manchester. There was no point in Bethan and Jess joining me on this trip; they would be better off at home.

It was an uneventful journey, with Radio Wales forecasting the usual bottlenecks as commuter traffic approached the larger towns. The Post House Roundabout was a familiar name to listeners to Radio Wales; now here I was, negotiating it, outside Chester as I turned on to the M56.

My sat-nav guided me accurately to the back street where stood the shop of Just Computers.

It was a street of dereliction. Empty terraced houses, their broken, unglazed windows and shattered doors showed that nobody cared whether the vandals got in; their lack of contents showed that the vandals had been in and were long gone, having no further interest in what had been neat homes for the mill workers way back in time. Either side of my destination had stood two buildings, probably shops from the size of their window openings, which had burned down, their charred timber-work witness to the fires which had miraculously left Just Computers alone.

I turned my attention to Just Computers

Hand-written labels in the dusty window proclaiming 'EVRY ONE GARANTEDE' would have benefitted from a spell checker, though the writer had had no trouble with 'CHEAPER THAN IN TOWN'.

A bell, a relic from the old days which nobody had bothered to remove, rang above my head as I pushed the door open. A man's voice from the back room told me that he would be with me in a minute, so I replied that there was no rush, then used the time to look around the shop. I suspected that it had been a grocer's in a past life, but became redundant due to the march of progress. Housing had been replaced with tower blocks, supermarkets had replaced the corner shops, leaving buildings like this ripe for re-development. I felt that the present occupier's days here were also numbered.

A mobile phone rang in the back room.

'Just Computers, Darren speaking,' said the voice, his conversation giving me more time to look around the shop.

The shop itself was quite spacious, with a door on the right-hand side of the far wall. This presumably led to the back room whence the disembodied voice had come as I entered and was now engaged in a complicated conversation.

The shop was about twenty feet square. The walls were lined with shelves, probably left when the previous occupier had departed. A trestle table, serving as a counter, crossed the corner in front of the back-room door. It was unlike any computer shop I had been in – not that I've been in many – but there were no printers, no monitors, no accessories of any sort on display.

Certainly, there was room for a lot more stock than I could see. A few PC's stood on the shelves and some empty boxes had been stored underneath the table. A quick examination of the labelling told me that they matched the boxes that I had seen in the lorry back at Llanynder.

'Right, then. What can I do for you?'

The now-familiar voice and its owner slowly emerged from the back room. A tall, thin, long-haired man in his late twenties, wearing jeans, a baggy jumper and some expensive-looking trainers, stood behind the trestle table. He had a friendly face, though experience had taught me not to jump to conclusions; that smile might be delusive,

'I'm trying to decide whether to get a laptop or a PC,' I began.

'I only deal in PC's, so I can't help with a laptop. It just depends. what you want it for.'

'Pleasure, mostly. Correspondence, emails, that sort of thing. And my wife is secretary of her WI, so she'd like something to help her keep things in order. So, just general stuff. No gaming or anything like that.'

'Well, there's pro's and con's on both sides. If you had a laptop, she could take it to meetings with her, on the other hand, if you had a PC, you would have no need to keep the battery charged up, for instance.'

'That's true,' I agreed, 'so what kind of thing are we looking at?'

'I can make up whatever you want, you know, memory, graphics, etcetera.'

It was time for me to play the innocent. I had already remembered to keep my right hand in my pocket. Two fingers missing would be too easily identified if anyone should ask.

'Oh, they're not all the same then? Looking round, I thought they were.'

'This is how they come in, and then I do all the tweaking to what the customer wants.'

'You seem to have had good sales lately. Not many here.'

'Nah, I had a load coming in but I've been let down. Story is that the lorry driver has done a bunk with my computers and the lorry. He's vanished. The lorry's vanished. And my computers have vanished, all hundred of 'em.'

'You must be doing well to buy in a hundred computers.'

'Yes, I was. I sell a lot on-line. Pandemic was good, because they all needed to work from home and took the chance to buy a new computer – paid for by the employer, of course. Then, when it was all over, people are starting up little businesses, so, again, a new computer is called for. I don't do peripherals. Too much trouble and they can get keyboards, printers, whatever they want cheaper on the net or in the supermarkets. But nobody can beat me on price, so that's where I stay.'

'I've obviously got something to think about. So has my wife.'

I said I would be back when we had decided.

'Well, don't be too long making your mind up. I'm moving from here in a few weeks.'

'But you won't be far away? Or will you?'

'No, the owner's moving me into the new precinct up the road. He's sold his properties on this street to another developer to pay for the new precinct.'

'He owns the precinct?' I hoped the surprise didn't show in my voice.

'Yes, and half of this part of Manchester, I think. You wouldn't think so, to look at him. Always wears a hoodie. Jeans and trainers is his style. He just looks like one of the lads. The casino up the road is his as well. He must be coining it left, right and centre.'

'If he's got a casino, I suspect he is coining it. That's where the money is.'

'It wasn't always a casino. He bought a closed down mill. Big building. Plenty of potential. All the houses around here were occupied in those days. He opened a bingo hall in the old mill. Bingo was very popular with the old dears who lived in the area and he was open every day. The council wanted the area cleared, so he told people some frightening tales about what the council was proposing and one by one he helped them out, as he put it, by buying their houses. Poor suckers didn't realise that it was their bingo money that enabled him to pay for their homes. Then a couple of fires in the shops nearby reduced the local services – there was a bakery on one side of this shop and a greengrocer on the other, both burned down. The hairdresser down the road left before her shop was torched, leaving nowhere to get a blue rinse, so the people started to move out. Gradually, the street was emptied until there's only me left.'

'So the fires were deliberate. How come? Why are you left alone?' I asked.

'I'm useful to him. I installed his computer system and I still maintain it. Which is why he's moving me into the new precinct. I'll be on hand for any emergency action if the computers go down.'

'But what happened to the bingo hall?'

'Well, because the people moved away into the tower blocks, he had lost his clientele. So he upgraded the hall into a casino. It was all part of his plans. He installed bars, restaurants, fruit machines. There's deep carpets and expensive furniture in the quiet rooms where people can relax. He's hot on health, too. No drugs, no smoking. Lots of Premier League footballers get in there with more money than they know what to do with. You can't move in the car park for Mercs, BMW's, and Porsches.'

'Will I have heard of him? What's his name?'

'It's doubtful. It's Curtis Jandrell.'

'You were right. I've never heard that name. What's the casino called, by the way?'

'The Dragon's Lair. It's just half a mile away.'

It was as well not to dig further. It might arouse suspicions, so I thanked Darren for his time, said I might return later, took one of his business cards and left.

Five miles driving up the road brought me to Denny Shaw Truck Hire. As I waited for the oncoming traffic to pass before I could turn right into the yard, three police cars with blue lights flashing pulled in ahead of me. I made an instant decision to move on and managed to find a parking spot on a side street fifty yards away. I had noticed the usual bunch of smokers outside the gates; they would be my only chance to ask questions.

'Bit of excitement?' I said, nodding my head towards the flurry of yellow-clad policemen swarming over the yard and into the office.

'Dunno what it's about,' one of the smokers replied.

'Unless it's that lorry that went missing, Joe,' one of his colleagues put in, a lad barely out of his teens.

'Why would they come mob-handed if Denny was suspected of anything. He could hardly steal his own lorry, could he? And why so many?' Joe sneered. 'Anyway, I never trusted Dan Brennan. He's driven a few trucks from here and he always looks twitchy; nervous, as though he's been up to something.'

What luck! This confirmed that I was on the right track.

'Denny reckoned Dan had pinched the lorry. It's been missing a couple of weeks now. He'll have had it re-sprayed and back on the road by now. Or sold it.' The imagination of youth!

I could hardly tell them what had really happened to Dan Brennan and their lorry, but before I could comment further, one of the police came over to the gate.

'We need all the staff inside. In the warehouse. Straight away.'

Cigarettes were stubbed out; hands went into pockets as the smokers did what they could to indicate their grudging compliance before shuffling off reluctantly to the warehouse.

'Are you staff?' the constable asked me.

'No, just a passer-by'.

'There's nothing to see here. On your way.'

I didn't argue, I made my way back to the car and prepared for the journey home. There would be no interview with Denny Shaw that day.

Nine

I don't know who was more pleased to see me when I got home that evening, Bethan or Jess. Bethan stood on tiptoes to deliver a passionate kiss as she held me in a tight hug that said more than 'welcome home' – it told me that she was glad I was back and the day had not been good. Jess, on the other hand, sat at my feet, looking up at me with those big, soulful, brown eyes, her mouth half open, tongue lolling out, tail wagging, 'welcome home' written all over her.

I reluctantly let Bethan go and bent to rub Jess's head between her ears and to make a fuss of her.

I had rung Bethan on the return journey and told her my sat-nav's forecast of my time of arrival, which coincided nicely with the arrival of a mug of tea as I perched on a kitchen stool. God bless Bethan. God bless sat-nav.

Forewarned by the hug at the door, I didn't want to quiz her about her day; it would come out in her own time.

'How has Jess been today?' was my way of opening a conversation.

'She's been very good. We had a walk this afternoon. Up past the chapel and back. Just half an hour, didn't we, Jess?'

Jess responded with a wag of her tail and Bethan stroked her fur, gently.

'You two are my favourite girls,' I said.

It was strange that she didn't enquire about my day. It was almost as though she felt that if she didn't mention it, it didn't happen. But why would she want to blank the day out?

'Manchester was interesting,' I began. 'Had a nice chat with a young man selling computers.'

'We're not having a new computer, are we? I thought the one we've got was enough for us.'

'Oh, it is. But you remember David wanted me to find out what I could? I just had to pretend that I wanted information before buying one. I even quoted you as part of the pretence. I said that you wanted a lap-top because you were secretary of the WI.'

Her face fell. 'Don't bring me into it, please, Hugh. I thought you were just finding out things for David, but it seems dangerous to me. Remember the last time?' Her lips quivered as she spoke.

I got off my stool and folded her into my arms. Tears rolled down her cheeks as she sobbed uncontrollably, pressing her head into my chest.

I could not make out why she was thinking this way. 'The last time' that she referred to was when she saw what had happened to Brenda after she had been beaten up by a couple of thugs. Then, shortly afterwards, her policeman husband had been killed. It was a time of violence in the valley and, yes, I was in the middle of it. She certainly knew of David's history and his theories about gang involvement in Sallie's death, but my visit to Manchester was nothing to do with that.

She tried to tell me something, but the words were unintelligible through the sobbing.

'Don't talk,' I said, soothingly. 'Tell me in a few minutes.'

I snatched a handful of tissues from the pop-up box on the kitchen work-top and gradually the tears subsided as she mopped her face dry.

She looked up at me and smiled; a little forced, I thought.

'I feel better now. It was just the relief when you came home. Jess and I were quite lonely, weren't we, Jess?'

Jess wagged her tail, unaware that she was an accomplice to an untruth.

'Bethan, you are kind, you are beautiful, you are helpful – I could carry on with the compliments – but one thing you are not is secretive. How about you telling me what happened today? I know there's something.'

Again, I took her into my arms as the tears restarted, for them to be quickly controlled with the help of more tissues. She hitched herself up on to a kitchen stool, blew her nose and began to tell me about her day.

'After lunch, I took Jess for a walk, as I said. We were out for about half an hour. I didn't see anyone to speak to. It was so peaceful. I was in the back yard, taking my boots off, when two men appeared in front of me. I didn't hear them coming. They were both big men. They frightened me, Hugh. Jess came out, barking, and they backed off. She didn't trust them. She kept growling. One of them said 'You want to keep that dog under control, missus.' I told him she was on her own ground, so what did he want.'

My mind immediately flashed back thirty years, to the day that Nell had died protecting me. It was happening again, but this time it was little Bethan and Jess who were in danger, not me. I reached out my left hand and held hers to give her the confidence to continue, as she was finding it difficult to speak between sobs and taking gulps of air.

'Take your time. No rush,' I said and gradually she calmed down and went on.

'He said he'd seen you at the pub the other night and he's heard you are involved with the police investigation of the lorry in the landslide. He knows about what you did thirty years ago and if you don't back off, he would be back and you nor the dog would save me.' She took in a lungful of air. 'What did he mean, Hugh? I'm so frightened.'

My mind was in a whirl. Who was he? How did he know my past? How did he know about my involvement with the lorry? What else did he know? How could I protect Bethan? And Jess?

'You were very brave, Beth.' I said.

'I had Jess to protect me. But it did take me back to the night that....' Her voice tailed off. She was still unable to recall that night after Lawrence's death without fearful emotions, the fear when two big men had taken Brenda, violently, from her. There were too many parallels.

'I don't know who these men were or why they would want me to leave it alone, though at a guess they might be involved with the illegals who were on board the lorry. All I have done is find the vehicle in the first place and I've sat in on the planning of its removal, and that is all. David wanted me to ask a few questions in Manchester, but nothing like investigation work and anyway, they couldn't have known about my trip today. As regards the pub, the only others in there when I was with David were two men from Manchester who David seemed to have seen before in his last job. I'll have to ask him more about them. So you mustn't worry. I wouldn't let anyone hurt you, Beth.'

Inwardly, I was worried. I had felt just as protective about Brenda and she ended up in hospital. There was a list of what I called 'rag doll bodies', a succession of limp corpses that featured in my life thirty years ago. Here we go again. Twenty Koreans and a lorry driver to start with. Who am I kidding when I say I will protect Bethan and Jess? They must be my first priority.

Bethan retired early that evening, her traumatic day having taken its toll, so I took advantage of the time to ring David. He answered on the first ring,

'How did it go in Manchester?' he wanted to know.

I related my conversations with Darren at the computer shop, about the failed delivery and confirmed that the boxes I had seen there matched the ones on the lorry. I included that Darren had also told me about his landlord. Curtis Jandrell, who owned most of the property in the area, including the Dragon's Lair casino. David seemed more than a little interested in that snippet of news. I then told him about the police raid on Denny Shaw's Truck Hire company and reported failure.

'It's just as well you were outside the gates. If you had been inside, you could have been implicated, arrested even.' he said.

'Something odd also happened here while I was away,' I said. 'Two men turned up here and threatened Bethan if I didn't back off. I suspect they were the couple you and I saw at *The Horseshoe* when we had a drink together. They couldn't have known I was in Manchester today, so where do they get their information from?'

David thought for a moment, then continued. 'That's a puzzle. I haven't mentioned you to anyone, if that's what you're thinking. I thought they may have recognised me, but I didn't think they'd seen you. I'll ring Gareth at *The Horseshoe* to see if he can help. I'll let you know how I get on.'

'I can't put Bethan or Jess at risk, so all I can do is back off, as they said. No more trips to Manchester, I'm afraid. I can't do it.'

'I understand perfectly,' he said.

'But tell me something. Do you know Curtis Jandrell? I sensed some recognition when I mentioned his name.'

'Yes, I know of him. He's an influential man in Manchester. A bit eccentric. Always wears a hoodie. I suspect he's involved in criminal activity, but nobody has yet nailed him down to anything. He came up there about twenty-five years ago. He bought a few houses in a period when the City Council was engaged in clearing out the old stock of houses and he converted an old mill into a bingo hall. That provided cash for him to continue buying up houses and he's now reaping the rewards of his investments.'

'He's obviously made a fortune,' I agreed. 'Darren at the computer shop said he's also built a new mall, - precinct he called it. Just Computers will be moving there soon. Darren does all the maintenance on the casino computers, as well. He's well in with his landlord.'

David went on. 'It's a pity you're giving up on this. I was going to suggest another trip to Manchester. No need to worry. It's nothing to do with the illegal immigrants. A lady I was at university with, Louise Sturgess, is a croupier at a casino. I'd like to get in touch with her again. The last time we were in contact she was working at the Golden Rainbow Casino in the city centre. What do you think?'

I thought hard.

'Leave it with me. I'll ring you back,' I said, and closed the call. But even hard thinking wasn't productive. I couldn't leave Bethan here on her own, even with Jess. I couldn't take her with me. Could I hide her somewhere? Crazy ideas floated through my mind. Two heads are better than one, so I decided to ask Bethan for her ideas. By now, she was fast asleep. It would have to wait until the morning.

Next morning dawned with a Bethan who had not entirely recovered from the previous day's problems, though she was quite cheerful on the surface. Over breakfast, I told her that I had spoken to David and that he had other tasks he was hoping to ask me to do.

'It's nothing to do with the Koreans,' I explained, to forestall the objection that I could see on her face was forming in her mind. 'I told him I was not leaving you here alone any more. Even with Jess,' I said. 'But I would like to help him if I could.'

Bethan looked thoughtful.

'All I would like is to run away, miles from these threats,' she said. 'Somewhere they wouldn't find me. Of course I'd feel safer with you, but I sometimes feel that tragedy follows you around.

Don't get me wrong. I love you and I do feel safe with you. Perhaps if I went away for a short time, you could sort out these problems and we could go back to our peaceful life again.'

'Well done, Bethan,' I thought. She had come up with a solution that I had hesitated to suggest.

'What if I give David a couple of weeks?' I said. 'I'll need to return to get the school ready for next term. You can go away for a fortnight's holiday so you'll be safe. Where would you like to go? North Wales?'

'No. Somewhere further than that.' She thought on. 'Jess wouldn't like Blackpool. Too many people. What about the Lake District? There would be plenty of walks. Lovely scenery. Yes. Somewhere in the Lakes will be great.'

I rang David to tell him of our decision.

'Wonderful idea,' he said. 'Try The Old Coach House in Carrsthwaite, I used to stay there when I went walking. Peaceful B&B. Wonderful walks, dog friendly, brilliant scenery; she'll enjoy it.'

We rang off for me to tell Bethan the news and to make an immediate start on preparing for her holiday. She was as excited as a child about the new arrangement, though she wished we'd be going together. At least she was happy at the thought of being safe. We agreed not to tell anyone where she was going; security was important.

Luck was on our side! A cancellation at The Old Coach House enabled us to book Bethan and Jess in for two weeks. Next morning we were on our way to Shrewsbury station for the journey north.

Bethan was more than a little apprehensive as we waited for the train. This was a journey she was undertaking alone. She was among regular travellers who understood the system and coped with changes of trains and of platforms on a regular basis. She was burdened down with 'what if's'. I managed to pacify her on most

56

things. 'Listen for announcements. If in doubt, ask somebody, staff preferably; other travellers will help if they can. If it's a real problem, you have your mobile, ring me. Get a taxi from the station. And enjoy yourself. I'm sure you will.'

A nervous kiss later and she was on the train and away on what, for her, was a big adventure.

Now at a loose end in Shrewsbury, I took the opportunity to call in at *The House of Kimchi*. I needed to see Grace and there was no better opportunity than when I was in Shrewsbury with only the journey home on the agenda.

I ordered coffee and asked if Grace was working today.

'She's on her break. I'll get her. What's your name? Don't keep her long.' Her boss was a surly man who was keen to let me know who was in charge.

'It's Hugh,' I replied.

And he vanished through the beaded curtain, his machine-gun burst of questions still echoing in my ears.

Grace's face appeared through the beaded curtain, her quizzical look changing to relief as she recognised me.

'Nice to see you again, Hugh,' she said. 'How is Bethan?'

'She's fine, thanks. I've sent her off on holiday for a couple of weeks to give her a break. I've just put her on the train, so I thought I'd come to see you while I'm here.'

'Have you any news about the people in the lorry?' she asked.

'Yes. We've had helicopters and excavators on the job and they have all been taken to a temporary mortuary in Welshpool. It's a bit more accessible than Llanynder. They were all dead, I'm afraid, but you knew that, didn't you? I think the police are starting their enquiries. I've been away for a couple of days so I'm not up to date with what's gone on.'

She looked at her watch and then, nervously, across to the counter, where her boss was keeping a watchful eye, - and ear - on us as we chatted.

'It's nice of you to come to see me, to keep me informed. They were my compatriots (is that the right word?). I'm the only Korean who knows they made it to Britain. I would like to go to their funerals if that's possible.'

'All of them?'

'Yes, all of them. I felt so close to Min-jun and his sister.'

'That's why I called to see you today. I would like you to write a letter to Mr Geldong. I feel responsible for the fate of his family. He needs to know where they ended up. Can I leave it with you?'

Another volley of Korean words sprayed machine-gun style across the counter and Grace said, 'I must go. Of course I'll do it. I'll let you know when it's done.'

Ten

I felt that my involvement in the landslide and the crashed vehicle had run its course. I had found it, reported it and assisted in its recovery. There was nothing more I could do. If it had not been for the message in the bottle, I would never have known about it, I would never have looked for it, and Denny Shaw would be scouring the country for a stolen vehicle, branding the late Dan Brennan as a thief. The truth was so tragically different.

Next morning, I rang DI Humphreys.

'Is there anything else I can do to assist you,' I asked.

'Nothing I can think of,' he replied, 'though I must thank you for all you have done so far. You have been invaluable, not just in tracing the vehicle, but your practical suggestions, such as the helicopter, as well. Your blacksmith friend was also invaluable. He was your suggestion, too. Your military training has paid off, albeit many years later. Many thanks indeed.'

'It's kind of you to say so' It was the best I could manage for a modest response, and went on 'There is one thing, though. This all started with a message in a bottle which was translated from Korean by Grace, a young Korean lady who works in Shrewsbury. It was a letter from one of the Koreans to his father in Korea. I have asked her to forward it to his father, with an explanatory note. I hope that's OK. I don't think the bottle or the note would be any use for fingerprinting. I had to wrap it in a towel to get a better grip

59

and the note has been in so many hands, including half a dozen children who all wanted to read it, that it would be useless for identification. I have a copy which you can have, with Grace's translation. The writer was the young man whose body was first out and he mentions his sister, who was the child in his arms when we found them.'

'I would like the copy, please, and the translation. Then my file will be complete. To bring you up to date, Greater Manchester Police have visited the hire company which owned the lorry. The company owner was relieved to hear that it had been found. He has been alerting as many other truck companies around the country as he could. He thought it had been stolen. However, he was not so relieved that he would be faced with a bill for disposal of the wreckage. Frantic phone conversations with the insurance company are ongoing, as they say. And that's about all I can say at the moment.'

'Thanks for that,' I said. 'Good luck with the rest of your investigations. Just one thing more. Would you let me know when the funerals of the Koreans will take place? Grace, my interpreter, is keen to attend. So are my wife and I. We feel close to these people. It's the least we can do.'

'I do agree. I promise I'll let you know.'

We said our goodbyes and closed the call. Now would be the time to ring David and hear what else he required.

The armchair in David's office had probably arrived there at about the same time as his predecessor, the long-serving Mr Day, had taken a post as junior solicitor with Mr Rhodri and Mr Jacson, both long deceased. It was extremely comfortable, as I found when I sank into its cushions, which smelt of furniture polish, and coffee, with a lingering hint of cigars from the days when it was possible to enjoy a smoke while discussing one's affairs with one's solicitor.

I was pleased that David had agreed to see me in his office. It was a chance to find out more of what was behind his almost obsessive interest in his past life in Manchester. Brenda West brought in two cups of tea with a selection of biscuits. I was sure that his normal clients didn't get this treatment. Obviously, we were in for a long session.

When Brenda had left and closed the door behind her, David began.

'I'm so pleased that you have decided to do the leg work for me. I really don't want to go back to Manchester at the moment, but I need these enquiries to be done. There are some that stem from the landslide and others which, shall we say, are more personal.'

'You mentioned a lady croupier last time we spoke. Where does she fit in?' I asked.

'She was a very clever lady, fresh out of university in those days. As she works in a casino, she picks up gossip about all sorts of players. I'm interested in the high rollers who would frequent casinos. Her information would be invaluable.'

'Why them in particular?'

'Because big money, very big money, is involved in much of the crime in the city and I would like to find out who's running it.'

'Which is leading us to … er…what exactly?'

'I said the landslide and personal matters were involved. Louise's information might lead us to whoever is trafficking immigrants, such as your Koreans; she might also help us to find out who killed Sallie, and why. You can see why I need you to do the investigative work. I'm too well known to the criminal community to do it myself.'

This explained his reaction to Red Rose Man that night at *The Horseshoe*. No wonder he didn't want to be recognised. But hadn't Bethan's visitors said that they had seen me that night? The head round the door, of course. I would have to be very watchful in Manchester.

David gave me the benefit of his homework. Red Rose Man, had, indeed, been back at *The Horseshoe*, on the day I was in Manchester. He had been up to the site of the landslide and had been chatting to some of the locals, both those sight-seeing around the site and in the pub at lunchtime. Obviously, I had been one of the topics of conversation. Locals like to gossip, especially showing off their knowledge to strangers and Red Rose Man had used that knowledge to frighten Bethan. David had also discovered from Court records, that Red Rose Man was known by the name of Gavin Scott and his mate was Ged Ross.

Their boss, recently released from prison, was Glen Dalby, who David had always felt would have a grudge against him, as the solicitor had been instrumental in Dalby's incarceration. His influence was in the north of Manchester, whereas Curtis Jandrell's sinuous tentacles infiltrated the south of the city. They were deadly rivals, each watching the other's movements, foiling their plans, upsetting their schemes, even killing each other's gang members in the many shootings that occurred in Manchester.

I could see why David was reluctant to return to the city to ask questions.

I would have to be watchful and careful indeed.

Eleven

My first job, when I arrived in Manchester, was to make contact with Louise Sturgess. All I had to go on was the Golden Rainbow Casino, north of the city centre.

I walked through the glass and chrome doors into a sumptuous foyer, the walls of which were adorned with floor-to-ceiling pictures of gaming machines with slogans such as 'Best Slots', glamorous croupiers under the heading of 'Live Dealer Games' and glittering couples enjoying a meal in 'Our Upbeat Restaurant'. It was a quiet haven with deep pile carpets and subdued music playing. I was met by Tilly, a short, blonde lady in her early forties. She had a pleasant manner, in contrast with the two Neanderthal security guards hovering near the doors leading to the gaming rooms, looking uncomfortable in their dark suits and bow ties, itching for some action.

I told Tilly that I was looking for a friend of a friend who used to work here. Is she still here, I wondered. It's been a long time since they were in contact. Tilly looked nervously over her shoulder when I said 'Louise Sturgess'. As the Neanderthals moved forward, she hurriedly waved them back and said, in a voice that was loud enough for them to hear, 'She's not here any more. She moved on. Let me show you out,' and took me by the elbow and turned me towards the door. Then, as we reached the door, she lowered her voice so that only I could hear, 'Try the Dragon's Lair' and closed the door behind me.

I had no chance of asking for an explanation. Louise was obviously not welcome in the Golden Rainbow but I was not to be given the reason why. And why did the Neanderthals move at the mere mention of her name? Did they expect me to get rough at the news of her departure? What had she done to earn their disapproval?

At least I had a lead. The Dragon's Lair, I had already learned on my previous visit, was owned by Curtis Jandrell. Had I wandered unwittingly into Glen Dalby's territory to cause such alarm?

These questions ran through my head as I drove across Manchester. I remembered to check my rear-view mirror frequently as I drove. I was conscious of the fact that I might be followed, though I didn't think they would have had enough time to report to their boss and conjecture about my motives for asking about Louise before deciding to follow me.

Next port of call had to be the Dragon's Lair. I parked in the car park there and walked up to the door.

Just as luxurious as the Golden Rainbow, Curtis Jandrell's casino was, if anything, a little busier. Curtis had come a long way from his days at the bingo hall. No pensioners with blue rinses here. Instead, well-heeled gamblers trod this deep carpet and ate at the dining room which offered a variety of cuisines. Premiership footballers came from all corners of the world and wherever they came from, they would find something from their homeland on the menu.

This time, though, I recalled my army training. 'More time on reconnaissance...' came to mind. Instead of rushing in with my enquiry to the first person I met – which had resulted in an early ejection at the Golden Rainbow – I opted for a gentle survey of my new surroundings. A pretty little receptionist, whose lapel badge told me she was Tracey, led me through to the bustling gaming floor and pointed out the live table games, where three-card poker and baccarat were in progress. The quietness of the poker room was a direct contrast to the noisy clacking of tiles and loud cheering from the four Orientals playing mahjong in the next room. Tracey asked if I had any preference for a game and I said that I would like to look around first to acclimatise myself. She pointed out the other facilities, though as everything was well sign-posted the guided tour was unnecessary, and she returned to her desk in the foyer.

From a seat in the bar, I observed what was going on through the large windows overlooking the gaming floor. Not all the staff had uniforms and name badges, I noticed. Some, like the striking brunette who was clearly the Floor Manager, wore maroon jackets. Dealers and croupiers were similarly attired. Waiters were in white shirts with a maroon waistcoat. But there were three others, observation told me, who were in plain clothes. Open necked shirts, jeans, with or without a jacket, not looking in any way 'official', blending in with the customers, observing with watchful eyes for any sign of trouble, or cheating or overt drug use or drunkenness. The only Neanderthals I saw were in the foyer, to dissuade any casual would-be customer from coming in if they were drunk or under age or both. The gaming floor did not need that kind of security. No-one likes to feel watched when they are enjoying themselves, though everyone knew that CCTV was operating and that there would be someone in a back room, seeing everything that happened. A visit to the toilet showed me that CCTV was literally everywhere, in the corridors, in all the gaming rooms, yes, even discreetly positioned at the restroom door, though not inside. There was no hiding place from the cameras.

At the end of the corridor between the bar and the toilet was a door which barred entrance to the admin area. Stern notices in many languages told me so. 'Staff only' really meant what it said, emphasised by the large gentleman seated adjacent to it. As I walked back to the bar from my toilet visit, I stood aside to allow the Floor Manager, the brunette I had noticed earlier, to pass, She smiled her thanks, but as she passed, I glanced at her lapel badge and saw the word 'Louise'. It was too much of a coincidence, but I quickly murmured 'Louise Sturgess?'

She stopped, turned, and asked 'And who are you?'

'A friend of David Pearce. My name is Hugh Evans. He needs your help about a case.'

She looked nervously at the cameras, both the one behind me and the one above the admin door at the other end of the corridor, and said, in hushed tones, 'I can't talk here. Go to the roulette table but don't speak to me.'

With that puzzling remark, she resumed her journey towards admin, with a cheery 'Thanks, Hal,' to the guard who pressed a button to open the electric door for her.

I made my way back to the gaming floor and watched, with other spectators, as the roulette wheel spun and spun, the expert croupier collecting the losing chips and rewarding the winners at the end of each spin. I must have been there for twenty minutes, during which time Louise had returned to the floor but had made no attempt to contact me nor even to look at me.

She finally arrived to stand next to me, under the pretence of checking that a small pile of chips was well inside its box.

A Geordie punter was doing well. His chips were mounting up and a small crowd gathered to observe a big win in the offing. There was some movement in the crowd as people craned to see the table and Louise was pushed closer to me. I felt her hand put a piece of paper into mine, then, as the Geordie lost his bet, the crowd eased and dispersed, disappointed not to have seen a big win. Louise walked over to the croupier for a word and I pushed my hand into my pocket without looking down at the paper as I walked away.

I was back in the car and well away from the cameras before I examined the paper. 'Cornwall Hotel, Didsbury 7pm tonight' was all it said.

Twelve

The Cornwall Hotel was housed in a Victorian town house in a residential street in leafy Didsbury, well away from the bustle of central Manchester, yet only a short drive away from the city centre B&B that I had chosen for my temporary base.

I waited in a quiet lounge, having arrived early so as to familiarise myself with my surroundings before Louise arrived. She was on time and we made our introductions quickly as we had already met, albeit briefly, at the Dragon's Lair, and made ourselves comfortable over a couple of drinks at a corner table away from other guests.

Louise was interested to know how I knew David. She knew he was Welsh but had gradually lost touch with him over the intervening years since University days. The last time she had seen him had been at his wife's funeral, but that was ten years ago. He had then immersed himself in his work and had neither time nor inclination for socialising. She was unaware, for instance, that he had recently left Manchester and returned to his roots.

I told her how he and I had renewed our friendship and that he had been the star pupil at the school at which I was caretaker. Her raised eyebrow told me she could not equate this, which led me to explain about my past at Llanynder and my involvement in the downfall of Colonel Llewellyn. David had shared my sorrow at the loss of Cathy; she had been his favourite teacher. Sometimes the brighter kids are left to their own devices as the teacher concentrates on the slower members of the class, but Cathy had always given David extra work to push him to his limits. He appreciated this; it was the foundation of the successes of his career since.

Louise was easy to talk to but then it was my turn to hear about her past.

'You went to University, but you've worked at casinos most of your life. How did that come about?' I asked.

'Yes, when I met David, I was at University, studying biology. My friend Sallie and I were inseparable and one evening in the Students' Bar we met a boy I was keen on, Steve, also doing biology. He and his friend David, a law student, were going out on the town and asked us to join them. Without going into details, you can guess what happened. We paired off, and eventually I married Steve and David and Sallie tied the knot soon after. We met up occasionally after that, until Steve and I found work in Australia. It was interesting work, on the Barrier Reef. We were both divers. It was our ideal job. But Steve tragically died in a shark attack.'

She shuddered at the memory as if she could still see his blood on the blue water.

'There was no way that I could stay there after that, so I came home. While I was at Uni, I had worked at a casino part time. On reception, mainly, but in the passage of time I became a croupier.'

I could see that she would have been an asset in either position, reception or croupier. She was stunningly beautiful. At the casino, her green eyes had been piercing, almost cold, and with her hair scraped back into a sleek top-knot, she looked efficient and business-like, but now, with her brown, almost black hair loose, framing a perfect face, her eyes took on a softer, more gentle appearance. A luscious red lipstick had been immaculately applied to her full lips, to complete the picture.

She went on, 'Soon after I came back from Australia, I went back into the casino and worked there ever since.'

69

She spoke the last sentence quickly, but I felt there was much more to it than 'worked there ever since'. Now was not the time to go into details; even a casual question would sound like interrogation, so I let it ride.

She continued. 'So, what can I do to help you? Why did David suggest you contact me?'

'David is convinced that Sallie's death was a punishment, despite the coroner's verdict,' I said.

'Punishment? Why does he think that?'

'He had been the prosecution solicitor when Glen Dalby had been sent to prison. It had been the result of his work that the prosecution was successful. He felt that it was tit-for-tat, a revenge shooting. Now some strange things have happened near home in mid-Wales. A lorry containing some illegal immigrants has overturned and everyone on board died. Then, a couple of men, who David recognised from his Manchester days, were asking questions at the local pub. He is sure there is a connection, and as Glen Dalby is now out of jail, David is feeling vulnerable, so he asked me to come here to ask a few questions in his stead. He thought you might have some ideas, as you hear a lot of things in a casino, with many shady characters among the clients.'

'How far have you got in your investigation?' she asked.

'I've found out a few things. For instance, I've discovered that Curtis Jandrell owns the Dragon's Lair. I'm not sure how ruthless he is, but some of his properties did suffer from suspicious fires. He's moved up from a bingo hall to a plush casino, making a lot of money in the process, and he owns quite a few businesses in the area, such as Just Computers, a shop which miraculously escaped the fires. And, of course, he's your boss. I'm sure there's much more for me to know. Perhaps you can help me. Incidentally, I first asked for you at the Golden Rainbow, but Tilly rushed me out when the bouncers started getting twitchy at the mention of your name. She told me where to find you. What's the background to that?'

'Well done, Tilly,' she said and went on 'Tilly was a great pal. When I worked there, we used to hang around together, just lunchtimes and the odd evening. We preferred a sandwich and a bit of gossip at the café round the corner to the exotic food that was served in the casino. When Glen was still inside, he had a manager.'

'That would be a responsible job for someone,' I commented.

'It was. Gavin got the job.'

'Gavin?'

'Yes. Gavin Scott. Big man. With a red rose tattoo on his hand.'

'He was one of the pair that came to our pub in Wales.' I said 'He didn't look like management material to me.'

'He was quite good,' Louise replied, 'except that he couldn't keep his hands to himself. He was after more than a quick fondle in the office. He cornered me, luckily by the desk, and, in the struggle that developed, I stabbed him with a letter-opener. Through his hand. I knew he was a violent man, so I had to leave. I grabbed my bag and coat and ran and never went back. He told Glen, still inside, of course, that he had found me helping myself out of the safe. Quite a few of the female staff had complained to Glen about Gavin in the past, so he was prepared to believe me when he phoned me from jail that evening. He even laughed about it. 'He was probably more upset about looking like wuss with a bandaged hand' he said, he just thought it was funny, but he could understand why I left. There were no hard feelings. But I don't think it's that way with Gavin's mates, the bouncers you saw there.'

I went to the bar and replenished our drinks.

'Is there anything else you can tell me about Curtis or Glen that might help me? Is there any kind of a war between them?' I asked.

'Oh, yes. They hate each other's guts. Story goes that Curtis put the police on to the drugs pick-up that resulted in Glen going to jail. The police reckoned it was worth a million pounds. Someone tipped off the police and the only clues to their identity were that the call came from the public phone in Curtis's bingo hall and the caller had a Welsh accent. As Curtis is Welsh, Glen assumed that he was the caller. He's hated him ever since and has sworn to get even.'

'So Curtis is Welsh?' I said. 'I didn't know that.'

'Yes, as Welsh as the hills and proud of it. Hence the name of his casino. The lair of a Welsh dragon. He's a strange man. Always wears a hoodie. Only one person I know of has seen him without it and he's dead, poor man.'

'What happened to him?'

'He was a window cleaner and he must have seen Curtis, bare-headed, through the window. It seems his ladder slipped and he fell from the third floor. He managed to say 'Curtis. Only...' before he passed out from the pain and died later in hospital. There were no witnesses. It was a windy day, and the window cleaner's mate, who should have been holding the bottom of the ladder, was hunched over, trying to light a cigarette between cupped hands, so he saw nothing and for that brief moment, he wasn't holding the ladder. Curtis's window was open, but he claimed that he only opened it when he heard the commotion outside and the ladder must have slipped because of the wind. Lots of us think he opened it to push the ladder, but there's no proof either way. We know he can be violent. And cruel.'

All this background knowledge was very useful. If so, it seemed that Glen was interested in the lorry load of immigrants. Why? Perhaps I had been barking up the wrong tree. Curtis

72

Jandrell might not be the mastermind I thought he was, though the consignment of computers aboard the lorry was expected at Just Computers, well inside Curtis's patch. What interest could Glen Dalby have had in that transaction?

We exchanged phone numbers and agreed that if I went into the Dragon's Lair, there would be no recognition.

'There are cameras everywhere,' she reminded me.

Thirteen

'Pull up a chair!'

Denny Shaw's offer of a seat on one side of his office desk was brusque. He told me, in no uncertain terms, that he was a busy man, so could allow me just ten minutes of his time to discuss my interest in a job.

'The sign outside your gate said you were looking for casual drivers, so I could be interested,' I said. 'I've recently arrived in Manchester and I could do with some employment.'

'HGV?' he barked.

'No, but I'm willing to learn. I was in the army some time ago and I drove all sorts of vehicles, including HGV's. My licences lapsed years ago. Even light delivery vans would be OK for me.'

'Could be possible, I suppose.'

I tried to change the subject. Imperative if I only had ten minutes.

'I called the other day, but you had the police in. A constable sent me on my way before I could get through the gate.'

'Oh aye. They're like that.'

I seized the opportunity to open the subject that I really wanted to discuss.

'Trouble, was it?'

It worked.

Denny was clearly stinging from the loss of a vehicle.

'One of our hire fleet had gone missing. Apparently, it fell off a mountain in Wales. What the hell it was doing there I don't know. Once a vehicle is on hire it's up to the hirer to look after it. The driver must have been barmy to go up there.'

'Local firm, were they?'

'Strange outfit. Some kind of an agent, but they pay well so I don't ask questions. There's just one guy who rings to book a vehicle. He's become a regular customer in the last couple of years. Safe Delivery, he calls himself when he rings. Seems to be something to do with importing. He goes to the docks a lot, according to the driver. And the driver always pays in cash when he returns the vehicle. Spot on. Without fail. Looks like I won't get paid this time, though. The insurance don't help either. They blame me for hiring it out. I should have known better, they said. Where's the paperwork? You're too trusting, Mr Shaw, they said. I won't be trusting them with my premiums in the future, mark my words. Then the coppers tell me that I have to pay for recovery. I said, 'Bury it where it is. Finish the job that God started. More bloody money.'

It was simple to see why Denny was a busy man. He was easily distracted, so that work mounted up as he chatted and poured out his woes, despite his initial appearance of efficiency. We finally got back to my future employment and he took my phone number and promised to get in touch when something suitable came up. Trusting.

It had been a useful interview, though. It was clear that Denny was not a people smuggler. Had he been one, he would have talked himself and his accomplices into jail at the first police interview. The name Safe Delivery rang no bells with me and a Google search later in my room brought up nothing useful. Furthermore, Denny had tried ringing back on the hirer's number, but his number must have been blocked, so there was no reply. The hirer didn't want to be identified, obviously,

Fourteen

That evening, I spoke to Bethan.

She was enjoying the rest and relaxation in the Lake District, though she was still a little apprehensive if spoken to by a stranger. Jess gave her the confidence to go out and they had some excellent walks together.

'How is your investigation going?' she asked.

I had to be honest as I was no nearer a solution.

'I'm still gathering information, so no breakthrough so far.'

'What about the lady croupier you mentioned. Have you found her yet?

'Yes. I feel she knows more than she's letting on at the moment. We'll need to meet again a few times before I gain her confidence. It's early days.'

'What's she like?' Bethan wanted to know, then suggested 'Wrinkled, bottle blonde, heavy smoker, mutton dressed as lamb?'

'Something like that,' I laughed. 'No, Beth, she's actually quite beautiful. Brunette, smartly dressed, she's floor manager at the casino.'

'Oh, yes. Behave yourself, Hugh Evans.'

'She's not my type, Beth.'

'And what is your type?'

'Five foot two. Blonde ponytail. Has a dog called Jess.'

'Good answer. Just you remember it.'

Relaxation in the Lake District was having it's effect. She was going back to being the Bethan I married, with a sense of humour. Her confidence was returning. Insecurity was vanishing. I stayed away from talking about my case, if such it can be called, to avoid reminding her about the two men who visited her at home.

Instead, I steered her on to what she had been doing. Carrsthwaite, it appeared, was a sleepy little village which she and Jess had explored in the first couple of days of their holiday. They had plans to go further afield; she had found a boat trip for tomorrow, a steam train trip for next week and a cottage serving cream teas on a circular walking route which they would visit more than once in the next few days.

I was pleased that she was so positive about things once more. I had no worries on her account. She was safe and happy. That's all anyone can ask for someone they love.

Fifteen

Next morning, I visited Just Computers. The derelict street was just as depressing as it had been on my last visit. Empty. Run down. Awaiting demolition. Not even a cat crossing the road. A logical progression into decay. No people, no food. No food, no scraps. No scraps, no mice. No mice, no cats. I parked in a space at the side of the shop and went in.

I thought a chat with Darren would bring me up to date with what he knew about the lorry. Darren, for once, was not engaged on the phone and we talked about the merits of his now depleted stock of computers.

'You told me you'd lost a consignment of computers last time I was in. Have you managed to trace them?'

'Yes. I heard that the damned lorry crashed and it all ended up in a river in Wales. You might have seen it on the news. The one with the illegals in. My computers were in that truck. Because of the rest of the, er, cargo, you might say, was illegal, it's doubtful if it was insured. And as it's treated as a murder scene, the police aren't releasing anything. I'll be moving into the precinct soon, so the owner said we'd hang on until then before replacing them. He's already put an order in to our Irish supplier. New shop. New stock.'

'Good plan,' I agreed. 'No point in moving stock twice. Get them delivered to the precinct when the new shop's ready.'

The silence of the street was suddenly shattered by the revving of a car engine as it accelerated towards the shop. There was a screech of brakes and squealing tyres as it halted in front of the shop. Shots rang out, followed by a hail of machine gun fire as the shop windows splintered and crashed to the floor. Memories of the Falklands flew through my mind and instinct kicked in as I flung myself to the floor, shouting 'Down!' to Darren as I did so. More revving announced the departure of the car as quickly as it had arrived. I raised my head enough to get a glimpse of it as it left. A black BMW. How anonymous can you get? I turned to Darren.

'It's gone. Safe to get up. You all right?'

There was no reply.

I ran across to him.

I felt for a pulse.

He was dead.

What was this all about?

Here I was. Alone in the shop. There were no other witnesses to the shooting. It's doubtful whether anyone would even raise the alarm. The empty streets had echoed the sound but no-one would be able to pinpoint where the noise had come from so it probably went unreported.

I took out my phone and dialled 999. I am only a customer, after all; there would be no need to reveal to the police my reason for being there other than enquiring about a computer.

The silence of the streets was once again shattered by the wailing of the police sirens. I waited on the pavement and stopped them before they reached the shop.

'What's up?' DI Natalie Thorpe looked annoyed at being held up by a civilian.

'It was a drive by shooting. There will be cartridge cases on the road outside the shop,' I explained,

'Thanks,' she said and strode into the shop.

She viewed Darren's prostrate body in its pool of slowly congealing blood. He had been shot twice, once in the head, once in the chest.

'How tall do you think he was?' she asked.

'About six feet,' I said, 'Same as me.'

She looked across to the police car now standing across the road and roughly confirmed the angle of trajectory from the car window. She already had a couple of constables outside putting up tape barriers and picking up cartridge cases, carefully marking the site of each one.

She turned to me.

'Are you the only witness?' she asked.

'Yes, as far as I know. The street has been deserted. I don't think he has many customers.'

She noted my name and address. I explained that I had visited Darren a couple of weeks ago with a view to buying a computer and had come back to find that a delivery of stock had not arrived.

'I was about to leave when this happened,' I said.

'His name was…?'

'Darren. That's all I know.'

'Was he the owner?'

'I don't think so. He did say his landlord was a Mr… Jandrell, I think it was.'

'Oh. Curtis Jandrell. We'll have a word with him. He'll need to board up these windows for tonight.'

'Moving these computers and the office stuff out might be easier. There's not much to move. It won't need much room.'

'You seem to be very knowledgeable.'

'Army training years ago. And Darren and I had long chats. Very talkative, he was. He also told me that he was due to move into the precinct soon, so moving everything out now would save a job later. If this place is due for demolition, I don't suppose the landlord would want to spend money on boarding it up.'

'Very true. I might put it to him when I see him. But we'll have a constable here overnight so there's no rush.'

'Can I go, then?' I asked.

'We'll need a statement from you first. For instance, what can you tell me about the shooting? What happened here?'

'Darren and I were standing here talking. A car raced up, screeched to a halt and the shooting started. I remember seeing someone leaning out of the rear window of the car with a gun in his hands as it stopped. Automatic fire. I dived for the floor and shouted 'Down' to Darren. The car raced off. I got a glimpse of the car, it was a black BMW, and went across to Darren. He was dead. So I dialled 999 and waited for you. I haven't seen anyone else in the street who could have seen what happened. And I didn't see who did the shooting, either. That's it, I'm afraid.'

'Can you describe the man you saw?'

'It was only a glimpse. He was white.'

'Hair colour?'

'He was wearing a black baseball cap. Peak at the front.'

'Clothing?'

'I could only see the sleeves, I think they were black, too.'

'Yes, she mused,' 'They're very careful not to wear anything that's readily identifiable, these days.'

She went on 'Could you come down to the station to sign a statement tomorrow?'

She patted her pockets. 'Damn. I haven't a card. Constable,' she called to a policeman who was on his knees examining a skid mark on the road. 'Give Mr Evans a card, will you?'

He handed me a card. 'The address is on there.'

'Yes, sure. Late morning?'

'Yes. It will be ready by then. You can go now, thanks.'

I left, the ancient door bell ringing in my ears for the last time as I walked around to my car.

What if I had parked in front of the shop? The gunman wouldn't have had such a clear view into the shop and Darren would still be alive with just broken glass to clear up. What if Darren had been on the phone in his office. What if the intention had been to frighten him and he was just accidentally shot? What if I had been killed? What would happen to Bethan? I must be more vigilant, though I hadn't been careless today.

Life is full of what-if's.

Sixteen

That evening I met Louise at the Cornwall Hotel to catch up on the day's events. She was full of news, mainly about a conversation she had had with Tilly when they met at the foot of the escalator in Marks and Spencer during their lunch hour.

'We had both been fitting in some retail therapy, which immediately took second place to a couple of skinny lattes as we caught up on each other's news. We compared our purchases as we chatted. Nothing exciting. Tilly had bought some new underwear, I had a pair of knee length boots for the winter, so that it was not long at all before we got round to the inevitable subject - work.'

She said that it seemed that Gavin was still being a pain. Apparently, he had cornered one of the cleaners, a Filipino girl, in the corridor and he was pushing her into one of the offices with the predictable intentions, when Glen came along. The girl ran off and Glen had torn a strip off Gavin in the staff restaurant.

It was unbelievable that it had been in the staff restaurant because all the staff there could hear.

Having been in that situation herself, Louise knew how the victim felt.

'What happened to the girl?' I asked her.

'Tilly heard she got a bonus from Glen, 'just to keep her mouth shut. And to keep her on the staff. He's lost a few because of Gavin, including me, of course.'

'And what happened to Gavin? Nothing apart from a telling off, I suppose.' I was still curious.

'No, but the problem is that he's got too big for his boots. Because he was running things when Glen was inside, he thinks he's the boss. Glen is having a real job to keep him under control.'

'But Glen's still in charge, isn't he? Does he still have that thing about Curtis and the Dragon's Lair?' David would be interested in her reply.

'Yes, he's in charge and probably still hates Curtis, but it's more like rivalry these days. Though Gavin was heard to say that he would show Glen how to run things. What that means we'll have to wait and see.'

Her lunch time news over, Louise sat back in her chair and said, 'So that was it.'

'I've only seen Gavin briefly, just a head around the pub door at home. What does he look like?' I asked.

'As tall as you. Well built. Strong - he does bodybuilding. Likes to show off to the ladies; he thinks he's God's gift to womanhood. And, as you know, he has a red rose tattooed on his right hand. That was my day, how was yours?'

'I went to Just Computers this morning to see Darren. I knew the company was owned by Curtis Jandrell and that Darren maintained the computer system at the Dragon's Lair. I thought that perhaps he could help me to find out more about Curtis's operations. We had hardly got chatting when a black BMW rolled up and sprayed the shop with bullets. Shattered the windows. I was lucky. I dived for the floor, but before Darren could take cover, he was shot in the head. He was dead before he hit the floor.'

Louise's hand went to her mouth as she uttered 'Poor Darren' and reached for her handbag to find a tissue to wipe away the tears which were filling her eyes.

'Did you know him?' I asked, gently.

'Yes. He spent a lot of time at the casino. There's a massive computer system there. Absolutely everything is done on computers. Security. The cameras. Accounts. Billing in the restaurant and bars. Membership. You name it. Darren was invaluable to keep it all running. He told me one day that all Curtis's other enterprises were also on this computer.

'Other enterprises?' I tried not to look too interested, but I had to know. 'Such as?'

'He owns a lot of property in this part of Manchester, so there are rents and maintenance. Reconstruction of poor housing areas, such as the precinct that's opening soon. The farm, a transport company, the computer shop...'

'A farm? That seems out of line with his other activities.'

'I don't know much about it,' she said, 'I just know he has one out on the moors beyond Oldham. I think he uses it for storage, not agriculture.'

Storing what? I wondered. Drugs, perhaps? Or would that have been the destination of the Korean immigrants? An old farmhouse would provide accommodation for a number of people. Human trafficking and modern slavery? This was getting deep.

I needed more information, but how to get it?

As Louise and I said goodnight I decided to go to Just Computers, on the off chance of being able to get in.

'I might call into the casino tomorrow. Don't worry, I'll be discreet,' I hurriedly added as a look of alarm crossed her face.

'OK. But be careful,' she said. 'Goodnight.'

I watched her tail lights leave the car park then raced to my car. I might just be lucky.

As I drove slowly up the still-deserted street towards Just Computers, I saw that the police tape was still up and a bored constable stood inside the shop doorway

'Hello, not much shelter there, is there, with the windows gone? So you got the short straw, then.' I said.

'Yes, and it's freezing.'

'Remember me? You gave me a card this morning.'

'I do, Mr Evans. Good memory for faces, and …er…other things.'

He nodded towards my hand.

'Yes, a bit of a give-away, isn't it?'

'I was wondering, could I have a look in the office for a minute? I won't take anything. You can search me if you like. I wanted to check whether he'd made a note of my address, just in case the owner wants to get in touch.'

It was a thin excuse, I know, but it worked.

'Sure, help yourself. There's nothing to take in this crappy little place.'

Darren's office was tidy, which was more than the shop had been. I looked for his diary, or an order book, and found both. Hopefully, he would have done work at the farm and would have its address here somewhere. The diary didn't help. Just a few entries about order and delivery dates. No work done for anyone else. Presumably, Curtis's businesses kept him busy. The order book seemed a little more helpful, with a list of work done. I flicked back the pages in time. As they flipped over, an entry caught my eye. *'CCTV in cage rooms only. Sperrymoor Farm* with*, thank goodness, a post code.'

I used Darren's pen to make a note on the back of an invoice which was lying on the desk and hurried back to the front of the shop.

'Thanks, then. All sorted. I'd say 'Good night' but it's not going to be good, is it?'

'You get used to it. The good part is that I'll get into a warm bed in the morning. The missus is a nurse and she's out of the house before eight.'

'So it's not all bad, then. I can say goodnight.'

He smiled a rueful smile and resigned himself to a cold, lonely vigil.

I went on my way.

There was a new puzzle in my mind.

Cage rooms?

Seventeen.

I drove up to the moors next morning, planning to spend the day on reconnaissance. It was a sunny day and the short drive up the M62 had been a pleasant change of scenery for a country boy, especially when I reached the moors, where sheep grazed and lakes reflected the morning sun.

I pulled into a piece of open ground, a lay-by or a passing place on this narrow moorland road, and took my bearings. Consulting the apps on my phone, I realised that I was getting close to my destination. I could see Sperrymoor Farm, standing on the opposite side of a small valley, and I reminded myself that today was observation day. It would have been easy to give in to temptation and drive on to the hairpin bend at the head of the valley and follow the road up the other side of the valley and past the farm, but observation from a distance would be the initial priority.

I looked around me and could see no other buildings whatsoever. Sperrymoor Farm was, indeed, isolated. You would need to be self-sufficient to live up here, I thought. A couple of large barns stood apart from the house, no doubt filled with ewes giving birth at lambing time, but my interest was in the house and its immediate surroundings.

My binoculars brought those into sharp focus. The farm house was built of stone; local stone, like the low dry-stone walls that edged the paddocks around the house and stretched up into the moors above. Tall, with large Georgian windows, the L-shaped house formed two sides of a square. Curtained windows prevented a view of the inside. My immediate thought was why the curtains would be closed at this time of day; there again, if it was unoccupied, the curtains would deter intruders.

The third side of the square was formed by a long, low building, formerly a shippon, I guessed, from the days when the building had housed a few dairy cattle, probably ten at a guess. A smaller building, which stood between the shippon and the house, had presumably been a dairy, but now its broken door hung at a grotesque angle on a single hinge and the corrugated iron roof was open to the elements where one of the sheets had blown off some time in the past. Broken panes in the only window completed the picture of dereliction.

Panning my binoculars slowly along the shippon for a closer inspection, I could see that there were no similar signs of dereliction. All three windows were soundly boarded up. The doors, there were two, were sturdy and new. Hinges and bolts were oiled. There were heavy padlocks on both doors.

However, there were no signs of habitation. No washing on the line. No cars on the yard. The small garden, once the provider of all a family's vegetable needs, was wild and untended.

As a further deterrent to visitors, the strongly made five-bar gate on the yard sported another heavy padlock.

I opened the car window and a gentle breeze was cool on my face. Outside, I could hear a solitary lark up in the sunshine. An occasional curlew called, while a red grouse appeared and then disappeared in the heather. There were no other sounds. No tractors on the fields. No traffic on the road. No aircraft overhead. Perfect peace. I settled down to keep watch.

Half-an-hour later, just when I was wondering if watching was the right decision, my phone buzzed. It was a text from Bethan. 'See what we've been doing,' it said. The attached photo showed a selfie of Bethan and Jess enjoying a boat trip on Windermere. I was glad that she was so relaxed and happy and said so in my reply. I'm not the fastest typist and concentrated hard to find the letters on the small screen of my phone. In my concentration, I had not noticed the white van approaching from behind me and continuing down to the hairpin bend at the bottom. By the time I had sent my text, it was climbing up the other side of the valley.

I picked up my binoculars as it pulled up outside Sperrymoor Farm. The driver unlocked the gate and drove on to the yard, then opened the door to the shippon building. He went in, then emerged carrying a long hosepipe which he attached to a tap on the yard before returning into the building.

Some minutes later, he came out, rewound the hose-pipe and returned it to the inside, then emerged carrying a large cardboard box, followed by another, both of which he placed in the back of his van. He then drove off, having re-locked all the padlocks on the way.

Cannabis was the word running through my mind. The hosepipe was a giveaway. The boarded-up windows confirmed it. Not only would they prevent anyone seeing in, but they would also prevent any stray shafts of light from escaping. Police helicopters passing over the moors at night would be unaware of the illegal horticultural activity below.

I had two choices. I could now go to the farm, fairly certain that I would not be disturbed, to confirm my suspicions. Or I could follow the van to see where it went and to see who else was involved.

I decided that the second would be the more fruitful, turned the car round and set off behind the van, fortunately catching up with it before it reached the motorway.

The van led me to a detached house on a lane outside Oldham. Hawthorn House stood well away from other houses; there were at least a hundred yards in either direction - a neighbouring house on one side and a demolition company's yard on the other - which had a variety of vehicles from staff cars to mobile cranes moving about.

The van driver had parked on the drive of the house and by the time I passed he was casting furtive looks over his shoulder as he took a cardboard box from the back of the van and carried it to the house.

I turned into the company's parking area. A big sign said 'Cross's Cranes', so I had better look as though I had some business there. I climbed the steps up to the office. This was in the upper of two portacabins which had been hoisted up on to a lower one which was used as a storeroom, thus saving ground space for the cranes to manoeuvre.

It was a dusty office, as one might have expected, with workmen in and out each day. The young lady seated at a keyboard looking intently at a screen looked up at me and smiled. 'Just a minute,' she said, then yelled down the stairs, over the noise of a mobile crane, 'Eddie, who's doing that one in Stockport?'

A distant voice replied, equally loudly, 'Jack Burnett.'

'But he's...Oh, I give up' The crane had won. Going into detail over that distance and at that volume would have been difficult if not impossible. She decided to wait for a more opportune moment to arrange Jack's schedule. She looked up at me again.

'Sorry about that. Why they have to rev the engines up like that, I don't know. What can I do for you?

'I'm going to need a boat lifted out of the canal in a few weeks and I'd like to know if it's something you do and what would it cost.'

'Yes, we lift boats regularly. As regards cost, it depends on the size of the boat and where it is.'

I glanced through the window and my attention was taken by a red Mini pulling up at the gateway of the house down the road.

'Sorry, daydreaming,' I said, bringing my attention back to the job in hand. 'It's about fifty feet long so it would weigh about eighteen to twenty tons, I suppose. I've only just bought it so I'm not very sure on details.'

'As a rough guide, depending on distance, it will be about five hundred pounds,' she said, 'but if you could find someone at the boatyard who wants their boat lifted out at the same time, you could share the cost of travelling between you.'

'Thanks for the tip,' I said. 'I'll bear that in mind.'

I glanced though the window again. The red Mini was still there.

'They've got a great view from that house, haven't they? All the way up to the moors. Good neighbours, are they?'

'I rarely see them. When the white van comes, they seem to have a lot of visitors. Always one car at a time. Eddie reckoned they were running a brothel, but they come as couples. Who takes his wife to a brothel?' she laughed.

'Very true,' I joined in the laughter.

I said my farewells and left, with a promise to let her know about the boat.

I drove slowly along the lane, hoping to see some activity at the house. I was disappointed. All was quiet. The two vehicles were still there. I drove on into the residential area further along the road and found a lay-by to park in, with a good view of the road, ensuring that I would be able to spot the Mini as it left.

Minutes passed; fifteen…thirty…forty-five…, during which I started to have doubts about the wisdom of sitting here, not knowing what was going on at Hawthorn House. Had I followed the wrong white van? There were so many of them about it would have been easy to make a mistake. Was it the same man, the same cardboard boxes, that I had seen up at Sperrymoor Farm?

Conjecture ceased as the red Mini came around the bend towards me. I made a note of its number and saw that the occupants were a young couple, obviously happy and smiling together as they passed. There was no way in which I could have stopped them to ask about their business at Hawthorn House. It was, obviously, their business.

I rang David.

'Hi. How's it going?' he asked.

'Quite well. I'm finding out quite a few things. Just familiarising myself with the territory.'

I didn't want to tell him I was nearly shot. That was a detail that could wait till later.

'I'm looking for a favour,' I said. 'Do you have a contact in the police who could provide an address from a car number plate for me, please?'

''Umm. Yes. I can try. I'm not sure whether he's still with Greater Manchester Police or even in the police after all this time but I'll try. Is it important?'

'Let's just say it will help the job along. I'll give you a full report when I come home. OK. I'll leave you to it. Must go.' We ended the call.

A blue Ford Focus had driven past me during my conversation with David and I was interested to see if it, too, was headed for Hawthorn House. I followed it. It was. As I drew closer, I could see it turning into the gateway to park behind the white van. Passing slowly, but not so slow as to arouse suspicion, I saw a young couple with a little girl, eight or nine years old, going up to the door.

I drove to the demolition yard again, to turn around and made my way back to the lay-by, but this time I parked on the other side of the road to face the Focus as it returned. An hour passed before the Focus came into sight. I leaned out of the window and waved it down. They pulled up and the driver wound his window down.

'Sorry to stop you. I'm not used to these country lanes,' I said. 'Is this the way to Hawthorn House?'

The driver, a smart thirty something, smiled and said, 'Yes, it is. Round the bend. About two hundred yards. Are you after a puppy as well? We've got a beauty. Well worth eight hundred quid. Show the man, Crystal.'

The little girl, sitting in the back seat, held up a sandy coloured spaniel puppy.

'That's lovely,' I said and she smiled her agreement. 'Did you say eight hundred?'

'Yes. She wanted nine hundred but I offered seven so we decided to split the difference.'

'You got a good deal there,' I said, hoping that I sounded encouraging. 'Nice lady, was she?'

'Yes.'

'You have to be so careful these days. Did you see the mother with the pups?'

'No. She said her husband had taken her to the vet for a check-up. I know what they say - be careful, and all that - but she was such a nice lady and Crystal had fallen in love with the pup - you know what kids are - well, I thought I could take a chance. The house was tidy and well furnished. My wife took Crystal to the downstairs toilet in the cloakroom and she said how nice it all was. Absolutely genuine. I'm sure we'll be alright.'

'Can we go home, Daddy? I want to show Rusty to Granny.' Crystal was getting impatient.

'I mustn't keep you,' I said. 'Thanks for stopping.'

'Yeah. Bye, then. Kids, eh?' and with a rueful smile he started to wind his window up.

'Before you go. How did you find out where to come?'

'Classified. Manchester Evening News,' he said, and drove off.

I backed up and turned around. Better not go up to the demolition yard again to turn around. The fewer chances of being spotted the better.

SPANIEL PUPPIES - Ready now. See them with Mum. Ring for appointment to view.

This brief advert appeared in the Manchester Evening News which I bought at the first newsagent I passed on the way back into Manchester. Scanty on information, I thought. No mention of vaccinations, upbringing or Kennel Club registration, which seemed to feature importantly in other adverts for puppies. Similar abbreviated adverts appeared with other breeds in the title. The only other difference was the phone number, which suggested a different seller.

I thought of a little job for Louise and rang to arrange a meeting at Cornwall House for 7.30. She seemed reluctant to turn out, but as she would be off work for a few days, she agreed, though she suggested we go to a different venue. She suggested Coco's, a little café in a side street in Stockport.

'Booth number three,' she said.

'Sounds a bit cloak and dagger to me,' I said, meaning it as a joke, but she replied 'It is. You'll see why later.'

I had to be satisfied with this cryptic reply.

Eighteen

During the daytime, Coco's would have been full of ladies, hair newly and stylishly coiffed, colourful nails neatly polished at the nearby nail bar, fingers dripping with diamonds, enjoying morning coffee or afternoon tea, depending on the hour. Red and white gingham tablecloths and dainty china crockery had been removed as the evening fell to be replaced by candles in bottles, slate placemats and silver cutlery on the bare, well-polished wooden tables. At the back of the room, away from the windows, were three booths containing tables for two, where couples could meet, safe in the knowledge that their conversations would remain confidential.

I was met at the door by a smart young man whose jet-black hair and neatly trimmed beard contrasted with his crisp white shirt.

He wished me a good evening, then enquired,

'Do you have a reservation, sir?'

'Booth number three?' I offered.

He consulted his iPad.

'In the name of Evans? Booked by your secretary?' he asked.

'That's me. Thanks.' I said, with a wry smile, as he led me to the back of the room and saw me safely into Booth Three. So Louise had booked this in my name, introducing herself as my secretary. I wondered why. Not that it was a problem but she must have had a reason.

He asked about a drinks order, but I said I would wait until my friend arrived.

'She won't be long,' I added, looking at my watch, which told me it was seven twenty-five.

Left alone, I took in my surroundings. The booth was surrounded by screens of ornate swirls of basketwork obscuring the view towards the window. My vision was limited to what was inside the café. However, logic said that if I could not see out, someone outside could not see in. My flip comment about 'cloak and dagger' had been closer to the mark than I thought. But why Louise had chosen this degree of secrecy was a mystery to me.

The other tables were filling up as diners arrived. A group of five or six made their way to a table nearby and as they took their seats one lady walked out of the group towards me. The hood of her coat was still on her head. I could see no features as she was silhouetted by a street lamp outside the door. Uneasy, I started to get to my feet, but she slipped into the booth and sat with her back to the ornate screen.

'Sit down, Hugh,' she said.

I still could not see her face, though I could tell that she was wearing dark glasses and a silk scarf covered the lower half of her face.

Recognition dawned.

'Louise,' I said. 'You surprised me. Why all the secrecy?'

She slipped back her hood, then removed her dark glasses, then lowered her silk scarf.

'We have a problem,' she said.

I sat back in amazement. Her left eye stared out from the black bruising around it. The left side of her face was swollen and a dull red. She had a huge blood blister on her top lip.

'Who did this to you? And why? How did it happen?' Questions tumbled out until I drew breath, giving her a chance to reply.

'Curtis,' she said quietly. 'This is why I wanted to meet here, in this booth.'

'From the beginning. Tell me what happened.'

'He called me into his office. 'Sit down,' he said. Two chairs stood, facing each other, in the middle of the floor. I sat on one. He sat opposite me, our knees almost touching. Two of his bouncers stood by the door. The atmosphere was threatening, even though he had said nothing yet.

I asked him if anything was wrong.

'Who's your boyfriend?' he asked.

'I don't have a boyfriend,' I said.

'You met him in the corridor,' he said.

'I don't know what you mean. I said.

'His right hand swung round and slapped me across the face. It sounded like a gunshot. I was knocked off the chair and lay face down on the floor. The bouncers picked me up, an arm each, and sat me on the chair once more.'

'Think again,' he said.

'I haven't got a boyfriend. I haven't met anyone in the corridor.'

Another slap put me on the floor again. The bouncers picked me up and returned me to the chair.

'Why are you doing this?' I asked him.

'I'll show you why,' he said and pointed to one of the CCTV screens on the wall. He stopped the action with the remote and I could see you and me in the corridor. He pointed out that I looked at the cameras when we spoke, then he changed cameras to show the roulette table and we were standing together.

'Now tell me that this was a coincidence,' he said.

'I've never seen this man before, honestly, boss. And I don't suppose I'll ever see him again. I thought you trusted me. What did you say when you took me on. Remember? 'We could do with a pretty girl round here,' you said. A pretty girl is always pestered for dates, boss, it goes with the territory. I could taste blood in my mouth. But I went on and said 'I'm not going to be pestered for a date any time soon, am I?' It was the only way to stop him, taking the battle to him, but now we know he doesn't trust me, we'll have to be careful.'

'I should never have involved you in this,' I said.

'No, I want to get even for this,' she indicated her face. 'He said that I couldn't work again until this healed up.'

'That's going to take time,' I said 'But it's mostly bruising, I think.'

'The heel of his hand caught my nose in that first slap, but I don't think it's broken. Otherwise, as you say, bruising will heal soon. But he will have me followed everywhere I go. Which is why we are here tonight. These people on the next table are my friends. I came with them and I will leave with them. Two of them will shortly go to the toilet. You will go with them. If anyone is watching from outside, they will not be able to distinguish you from the group and you can go out of the back door without being spotted.'

I was impressed with the organisation that Louise had set up to keep our meeting secret. She embodied a thought that I have always held. If you are dealing with criminals you have to think like a criminal.

'I wanted to ask you a favour,' I said, and went on to explain my thoughts about the adverts in the newspaper.

'There's a series of ads for puppies in the classifieds which give no information about the pups but they have different phone numbers. It's no good me ringing all of them. If they are all the same person, they would recognise my accent and get suspicious, but if different people ring them, they would just be congratulating themselves on a successful ad campaign. I'm just collecting information for David; I'm not here to join in any gang warfare.'

'Right. We have a bunch of volunteers to hand,' she said, trying to smile without pain, indicating her friends, 'They'll love this.'

I went on.

'Tell them to get as much information as they can - where to see the pups; age; vaccinations; make it sound as though they are a genuine enquiry; but not to give their names and to hide their phone numbers. We don't want any repercussions.'

'We'll have it done in the morning. It's time to go now. Tim, Terry. Toilet time.' she said over her shoulder to her friends. She had obviously primed them beforehand and they obeyed immediately no doubt enjoying the cloak and dagger approach.

Two of the group, both taller than I am, got to their feet and I slipped in with them as we went down a corridor. They turned into the toilets. I carried on through the kitchen and out through the back door, passing an open-mouthed chef on the way..

I would have to wait for results from their enquiries until tomorrow. I just hoped that Louise's injuries would heal quickly.

Nineteen

I was back in the B&B by eight o'clock, so I rang David with an update. It upset him to hear that Louise had been injured and asked me to pass on his concern. He expressed the hope that she would soon be mended.

'This is the problem when dealing with men like Curtis Jandrell,' he said. 'More often than not, they think with their fists. Which is why Curtis has to employ a sharp accountant to deal with his money. And there's nobody sharper than Archie Moffatt.'

'Who's Archie Moffatt?' I asked slowly, expecting that I would be hearing things that were way out of my experience and probably well above my head.

'I'll email some notes I made about him, so you'll know what you're dealing with if you come across him. Curtis has so much money coming in, not all of it legal, that he needs an adviser like Moffatt to make it legal, and to hide most of it from the tax-man.'

'Like money laundering, you mean?'

'Yes. Exactly.'

'Where does his money come from?'

'He arrived in Manchester with lots of money. Nobody knows where he came from and nobody knows where his money came from. But there was enough of it for him to start buying up these old properties that would be due for demolition when the council made up its mind to rehouse the people in tower blocks. He opened a bingo hall in an old mill. This provided him with a cash income, a huge cash income, so popular had it become.'

'Then he opened a casino?' I put in.

'Yes. How did you know?'

'Darren told me at the computer shop.

'Darren?'

'Yes. The intended recipient of the computers in the lorry at Mynydd Mawr. He's not with us any more. A drive by shooting. I was in the shop at the time. I wasn't going to tell you. You'd only worry. I didn't get so much as a scratch, by the way.'

I tried to gloss over the event. I don't like people worrying on my account and it was true, I was unharmed. I quickly went back to the conversation.

'How did the casino help him to launder money?' I asked.

'All the income is unrecorded. No receipts, no invoices, no paper trail. He can take money out and bank it elsewhere. It's the same with his other enterprises. He still has rents from houses, which are recorded diligently and properly, to give the impression of an upright businessman sticking to the rules. He owns a number of small businesses. Just Computers, for example. The paperwork said seven hundred computers were sent, but only about a hundred were actually on board, so a bit of false accounting is going on. He also owns the Irish company which sent the consignment. There's the money from trafficking, which it seems he's deeply involved in. That's new to me, but that money has to be cleaned somewhere. He would need a financial genius to launder and control all this money. If you are looking for a financial genius, Archie Moffatt is your man.'

'You might be able to add another illicit source to your list. Sperrymoor Farm, up on Saddleworth Moor. I've been up there; just a recce,' I hurriedly added then went on 'but I feel there's something going on there that I'd like to know more about.'

'I hope you're not putting yourself in danger, Mr Evans.'

'Course not. I've been very careful. And isn't it time you started to call me Hugh?'

'You'll always be Mr Evans to me, but I'll try.'

I could imagine the wry smile on his face as he said that. We chatted on for a few minutes, then finished the call. Two minutes later my phone pinged. David's email had arrived.

Archibald James Moffatt left university with a degree in Business and Financial Management. In the long vacations, he had volunteered for work as an intern in Accountancy firms, so that on leaving formal education he was able to start his journey up the ladder to qualified accountancy.

By the time he was thirty, he was a skilful, much-sought-after Financial Manager.

The peak of his career was reached when he was head-hunted by the Serious Fraud Office, where his expertise ferreted out many lucrative, but illegal, business ventures.

He had inherited his father's penchant for figures, though Jack Moffatt had never aspired to the heady heights that his son attained. Jack's bookmaking pitches were to be seen at all the racecourses in the country. It was when, as a child, assisting his father, running bets to local pubs, that Archibald acquired an interest in money. This was the driving force behind his career through university and accountancy to a top government post in the SFO.

He took early retirement to lead an ostensibly comfortable life in a small mansion in the footballer belt of Cheshire. Golf twice a week; season tickets at two Premiership football clubs; occasional visits to a casino; life was indeed comfortable. No-one begrudged him his Rolls Royce.

However, armed with the knowledge gained from his work at the SFO - which opportunities to follow, which pitfalls to avoid - he once more prospered as a Financial Adviser, but this time outside the law. Offshore bank accounts were bread and butter to Archie, as he had become known. It was Archie who had advised Curtis Jandrell to avoid drugs. 'Too many people involved, from the kids on the street, through dealers, up the ladder to you. Stay clean and the police will leave you alone,' he had said, and it had worked. Curtis's 'no drugs' policy had gone down well with his customers; there were no police raids; the reputation of his casino was impeccable as a result.

Archie counted Curtis Jandrell, Glen Dalby , a shady racehorse trainer and a couple of drug dealers among his clients. He therefore controlled most of the dirty money in Manchester.

David had added a note at the end.

By the way, Louise might be able to give you more information about Archie as he's a regular visitor at the casino.

This man sounded very interesting and I wanted to meet up with Louise to fill in what information about him as I could. I decided to ring her tonight to set up a meeting, though it might be difficult if she was being shadowed. We should not be seen together; that would only add to Curtis's suspicions, though I couldn't work out why he would be regarding me as any kind of threat. Surely Louise was allowed a 'boyfriend', as he described me, without interference from her boss?

She answered the phone after three rings.

'Hello?' She sounded guarded, hesitant.

'Hi. It's Hugh,' I replied quickly, to put her at her ease. She sighed her relief, audibly. Her voice went into relaxed mode as she told me that she was wondering who would be ringing her at this time of the evening.

'You thought it might be Curtis exercising his duty of care as a responsible employer, I suppose?' I joked.

'I doubt if Curtis has ever heard of a duty of care,' she replied, 'and don't make me laugh, Hugh. My mouth still hurts, even when I smile. So what can I do for you at nine o'clock on a foggy night?'

'David has sent me some information about Archie Moffatt and he says that you could perhaps give me some up-to-date information about him.'

'You could come round here tonight if it's urgent. I'm not doing anything. Just watching telly. You're not far away. Ten minutes in the car. But don't park at the front in case I'm still being watched. If you turn off our road into Merlin Street, you'll see a back lane on your left leading to the rear of the houses. Mine is number 5. I'll unlock the back gate before you get here. Is that OK?'

'Perfectly,' I said. 'I'm on my way.'

Twenty

It took fifteen minutes to drive to Louise's house, due to the dense fog. I had driven slowly and lost a few minutes finding the back lane off Merlin Street. The gate to Number 5 was well marked and the conservatory door opened as I walked up the path.

'Come in. I didn't realise the fog was as bad as this,' Louise said as I approached.

'It slowed me down a bit, but I managed,' I said.

Once inside, with the door closed against the chilly air outside, I looked at Louise's face.

'I see what you mean about not laughing,' I said. 'It must be painful. David asked me to pass on his concern about your injuries. He's worried about you.'

I wondered whether there was any more to their relationship. After all, she had come back from Australia a young widow; he had lost Sallie in brutal circumstances; they had been friends since University days; it wouldn't have been surprising if they had got together. None of my business, of course, but I couldn't help wondering.

I sat on a two-seater sofa in her stylish lounge. Louise sat opposite me on a matching sofa. Between us stood a glass-topped coffee table. Modernistic standard lamps stood in two corners of the room, their uplighters illuminating the ceiling and bathing the room in a gentle light. The TV set, now muted, threw a flickering light into the room, its brightness dependent on the progress of the drama on screen.

Suddenly, the doorbell rang.

Louise froze. 'Hold on, they might go away,' she said.

Loud knocking followed.

'No such luck,' I said.

'You go into the kitchen, in case it's one of Curtis's men. I'll open the door,' Louise said.

I slipped into the kitchen as bidden as Louise walked down the narrow hallway and opened the front door. I could hear that as the catch was released the visitor pushed the door open.

'Gavin! Get out! Don't push!'

'Out of my way. I'm coming in.'

'What are you doing here?'

'Get the door shut!'

'What do you want?'

By now, I could tell that they were both in the lounge.

'I've come with a warning. From Glen. He thinks you've been telling Jandrell about his business. You left in a hurry and since then things have been going wrong, business wise. We're losing customers at the casino in large numbers. Most of the Premiership footballers have moved out.'

'You can't blame me for that. We're not bribing them to come to us. None of them has said that he moved over because I did.'

'Well, Glen is doing his nut over the takings and he's blaming you. It looks as though you've had a pasting already. If you carry on, he could do a lot worse. He always liked you, that's why he sent me with a warning. Jandrell had a warning but he took no notice, so his computer man got shot. Just watch it in future. You might be next.'

'Tell him I've done nothing to damage his business. And who gave you my address anyway?'

'Tilly.'

'I told her never to tell it to anyone.'

An evil grin crossed his face.

'She didn't want to, but she changed her mind.'

'What did you do to her? You've bullied her into it, like all the other people you've bullied. It's time you left. Go!'

'I'll go, but I think we have some unfinished business.' He moved towards her. 'Remember the day you left?

'Get your hands off me!'

'You heard what the lady said.'

My voice echoed down the empty hallway. I had heard enough and could tell where the conversation was leading. I burst from the kitchen into the lounge and was in time to see Gavin throwing Louise on to a sofa. I came up behind him and before he could turn round, I took him by both shoulders and thrust him towards the hall doorway. I had seen the results of fighting in a living room many years ago when my own living room was trashed, so I wanted to avoid a similar result here. He turned around, eyes blazing, and swung a fist at my head, missing by a mile. I closed in and pushed him towards the door. He came at me again, but I clamped my left hand on his windpipe and again gradually pushed him, now gasping for air, along the hall. I unlatched the door with my right hand and pushed him out, staggering backwards down the path. I slammed the door behind him, making sure that I was not visible to Curtis's watchers, if they were still out there.

'So that was Gavin,' I said as I returned, more of a statement than a question.

'Yes. Thanks for coming in when you did. He's a nasty piece of work, isn't he? I hope he wasn't too rough with Tilly for her to give him my address. I hope she's all right.'

She led the way into her neat little kitchen, saying that she needed a stiff coffee after all the drama of Gavin's visit. She poured two cups from her machine and we returned to the lounge.

We had not even started to discuss the reason for my visit when Gavin had rung the doorbell, so I took my phone out and found David's emailed notes on Archie Moffatt. I handed the phone to Louise to read it for herself.

'A comprehensive set of notes,' she commented when she finished.

'So, do you know Archie well?' I asked.

'Fairly well,' she said. 'He comes to the casino regularly. Thursday nights. There's usually a Premiership match for him to go to earlier in the week. Plays a little poker. Nothing serious. Seems to have a limit on his spending. Doesn't play when he comes in on a Friday morning, though. That's every Friday. He has his brief case with him and goes into the office to talk to Curtis. Looks very official. No one is allowed in while he's there, Hal makes sure of that.'

'That's the guy in the corridor,' I recalled.

'Yes.'

She continued. 'Archie plays golf with the Police Commissioner on Mondays and Wednesdays. He seems to have a well-ordered life. That's about all I know about him.'

'Why do you think he calls at the casino on Fridays?' I enquired.

'I think it's to do with money. I know Curtis pays some staff weekly, so that's when he does the wages. But I can't imagine that Archie is necessary for that. Probably to do with banking. There's an awful lot of cash to be banked, even though more players are now using cards to pay. This information from David confirms that. He's a Financial Adviser so that must be what he's doing – advising Curtis what to do with his money. I wouldn't be surprised if money laundering is going on.'

'Money from his other enterprises may be in cash,' I said, 'so that might be brought in.'

'Can you remember if there is anyone who comes in regularly with bags which might hold cash?'

'Nobody I can think of, though Hal's wife, Bella, does some cleaning in Curtis's office. He won't let the other cleaners in there. She usually carries her cleaning gear in a Tesco Bag for Life. But nobody else comes to mind.'

'That's odd,' I said.

'What is?'

'Why does she need to bring in her own cleaning materials? Surely Curtis has a supply of stuff for all the cleaners to use.'

'That's very true. He does. I'd never thought of it like that.'

'I'll be interested to hear what your friends will report in the morning. You gave them a full briefing on what to find out, didn't you?'

'Yes. They will all be enquiring about a different breed and they'll ask all the questions you suggested. They'll ring at decent intervals throughout the morning.'

'Great. I'm looking forward to tomorrow afternoon. You'll let me know when they've rung?

'Of course. There's no point in you coming round here in daylight with Curtis's watchers outside. I'll email you with their comments as soon as I have them.'

I left the way I came. Tomorrow couldn't come quickly enough.

Twenty One

Next morning, I made my way up to Sperrymoor Farm once more. From my previous vantage point I could see across the misty valley that there was no white van or other vehicle at the farm. I waited another fifteen minutes, but as there was no movement, no sign of a resident, at the farmhouse, I drove quietly down to the hairpin and up the other side of the valley. I parked outside the still padlocked five-bar gate.

I climbed over the gate and walked up to the house, remembering that Darren's note had said that CCTV was in the cage rooms only. I just hoped that was accurate.

Yesterday's lark had lived up to its reputation as an early riser and was singing away above me but there was no other sound, other than the crunch of gravel beneath my feet.

I approached the house. The curtains were still closed on all the windows facing the road. Round the back needed no such security. Dusty windows, festooned with cobwebs, allowed me to see that Sperrymoor Farm was uninhabited. A huge iron range stood, rusting, on one wall of the kitchen. Another wall was home to a huge dresser, now devoid of the willow pattern plates, bowls, dishes and tureens which must have adorned its polished shelves; its cupboards were empty, with no sign of the bountiful supply of goodies that once enhanced the baking that went on here. Iron hooks studded the ancient beams, no longer supporting sides of bacon or legs of lamb, as in the old days when this kitchen had been a warm and welcoming centre of the farmer's operations and family life.

I moved on, coming to the narrow entry between the house and the dairy with its swinging door.

Having done an almost complete circle of the house, I was now back on the front yard, approaching the shippon. As I stepped on to the gravel path, the sound of my approach was accompanied by loud barking from inside the building. The voices of a large number of dogs filled the air, no doubt expecting the crunch of gravel to be the precursor of feeding time, as there was a human outside. High pitched and deep booming and all frequencies in between. This represented a large number of dogs. Hardly guard dogs protecting a cannabis operation as I had thought.

The strong smell of ammonia was a clue to the poor conditions within, almost making my eyes water when I was close to the doors but I could not see any way that I could inspect the interior. I looked again at the outside of the frontage. The windows and doors were securely boarded and locked. I had established that on my first visit. As it had been a shippon, there would have been no windows on the back wall. Was there a side door for cattle to enter and leave towards the fields? Or an internal door connecting to the dairy? It was worth a try.

As I pulled open the creaking door of the dairy, I could see that it was the repository for all manner of disused machinery and utensils. Ignoring the dust and grime of ages and with the encouragement of the sight of a door which hopefully led to the shippon, I started to make a path through the jumble. An ancient milk cooler, a dolly tub and a posser were all easy enough to move. Rusty garden tools, their handles worm eaten, took no shifting at all. A domestic mangle was not so easy, but I managed to by-pass it as I reached the door. The flaking lime-wash took to the air as I pulled it open. I coughed and sneezed as the white cloud combined with the dust which was raised by the draught of warm air which came through the opening. The stinging smell of ammonia once again made my eyes water, stopping me in my tracks.

The cage room.

The memory of Darren's note was enough to stop me from walking further into the building, avoiding the CCTV.

The noise was deafening as the dogs again gave tongue. I was unprepared to see row upon row of caged dogs, some with pups, some looking dejected, all looking ready for breakfast. Some young pups, smeared with faeces, were chewing the bars of their cages. This was not a futile attempt to escape, however; it was the result of boredom. I had seen the same kind of behaviour in pigs and horses. It's called crib-biting in horses. Other pups played with torn-up, urine-soaked newspapers which lined their cells. The whole impression was of a neglected, filthy, stinking mess – which was not an environment for any dog to live in. I closed the door sadly, thinking of my Jess's life of freedom and cleanliness and love.

The canine chorus subsided as I walked away from the building, though it was a sound I would find it difficult to forget. It would prompt my course of action for a long time.

Back in the car, I decided to visit Hawthorn House, to see what else I could find there. Thirty minutes later I was in the lane outside Oldham, checking my surroundings before approaching the property.

Again, there was no-one about, so after fruitlessly knocking on the door, in case someone was at home, I took the opportunity to look into the windows. The curtains were closed, so I tried the back of the house. Large French doors with, obligingly, no curtains, allowed me to view the lounge, which was sparsely furnished. The furniture looked as though it had come from a second-hand shop; the addition of a couple of colourful throws helped to make it more presentable, but not much. The kitchen, however, was a different kettle of fish. Sparkling appliances adorned every surface. A Tassimo coffee machine, a triangular red kettle and a Kenwood food processor all stood out on a green Westmoreland slate work top which matched the pale green cupboards above.

I had seen all I needed. Fortunately, David's contact in Greater Manchester Police had come up with the name and address of the owner of the red Mini which I had seen at Hawthorn House on my first visit, and I racked my brains for a method to approach him without having to divulge how I had tracked him down. Slowly, a plan formed in my mind and I drove off to see Ben Kealy.

The red Mini was on the drive of the address I had been given and as I drove slowly past, the young couple I had seen before, presumably Ben and Charlotte Kealy, came out of the house and prepared to leave in the car. She was carrying a Yorkshire Terrier pup, which sat on her knee as she fastened her seat belt. They reversed out on to the road, then drove off, overtaking me as I signalled to turn into a drive with a For Sale sign attached to the gatepost, trying, unnecessarily as it turned out, to make it look as though I had business there as a prospective buyer. At a decent interval, I continued after them, keeping a reasonable distance behind, and followed them into a Tesco supermarket car park.

I parked some distance away, watching for an opportunity to make a casual acquaintance.

Ben and Charlotte both went into the supermarket, with the pup tucked into Ben's jacket.

I was still thinking I had missed my chance as they emerged later with their shopping, put the bags in the car, then turned and walked to the neighbouring coffee shop.

I followed and found a table close, but not too close, to theirs. A family were on the table between us.

'Aw, isn't he cute?'

114

Two little girls on the next table, no more than ten years old, spotted the pup peering out from Ben's jacket and went over to him.

'Can we stroke him?'

'Of course.' Ben said, taking him out of his jacket and sitting him on his knee.

'Be gentle, girls,' their mother warned, as the girls took it in turns to stroke the little bundle of fur.

'What's his name?' they wanted to know.

'Tinker,' Charlotte replied. 'We thought he looked like a little tinker, so that's what we called him.'

The girls were full of questions – What does he eat? How old is he? How big will he be? – all the time stroking Tinker and tickling him behind the ears.

'Come along, girls. We've got shopping to do. Say goodbye to Tinker.' They complied, thanking Ben and Charlotte and blowing kisses to Tinker as they went.

'You've got a fan club there,' I said across the space vacated by the girls.

'It's happening all the time,' Charlotte said, 'but he is so cute, isn't he?'

'Do you mean me or Tinker?' Ben laughed.

'Tinker, of course, Ben. This is real animal attraction,' Charlotte joked back.

'Fifteen love, there, I think,' I said, 'But seriously, he is a lovely pup. Where did you get him?'

'There was an ad in the paper so we went up near Oldham to see him. Charlotte has wanted a dog for ages – well, since we got married - and as soon as she saw him, there was no going home without him.

'Was it a dog's home? Obviously not a rescue dog at his age.'

'No, a private house. Very swish new kitchen. Lovely lady. Bella her name was. She said her husband wanted eighteen hundred pounds for him, but because Charlotte was so taken with him, she reduced the price to fourteen hundred. That's good for a Yorkie.'

'Her husband wasn't there at the time?' I asked.

'No, Bella said that he'd taken Tinker's mum to the vet, so we couldn't see her.' Charlotte put in.

I finished my coffee.

'Well, I must be going. Nice to have met you. Good luck.'

As I left, I hoped they wouldn't need luck, that Tinker would have a long and happy life anyway.

You never know.

Twenty Two

I stopped at a pub, *The Rising Sun,* for a bite of lunch and somewhere to read Louise's email when it arrived.

A pint of beer and a ploughman's lunch were satisfying. I idly wondered how long it had been since a ploughman had been in that part of the country. Any fields around here had been turned over to concrete and tarmac many years ago. The atmosphere in the pub, however, was quite homely. The TV was audible but not intrusive. The bar staff were attentive. Customers chatted quietly.

The lunchtime news programme was followed by the regional news. I looked up suddenly at the mention of a familiar name by the presenter.

...a receptionist at The Golden Rainbow Casino. The body of Matilda Bolton, aged 40, was found on Carter's Mill Road in the early hours of this morning. Police are asking for...

That had to be Tilly. I rang Louise. She answered after two rings.

' Hi. It's Hugh. 'I said. 'I've just been watching the local news. Have you heard...'

'About Tilly? Yes. It's awful. Gavin must have gone too far this time. I'm sure it's him.'

She broke down into tears,

'What should we do, Hugh?' she asked. 'Remember what he said? 'She didn't want to, but she changed her mind.' With that

117

horrible grin. I wonder what changed her mind. She would have finished work at ten o'clock last night He left here just before ten in a terrible mood after you threw him out. I'm sure it's him.'

'Why don't we leave it until later? I can come round to you after dark and we'll discuss it then. What do you think?'

'Good idea,' she said. 'I'm too upset to talk to anyone, especially the police, at the moment.'

'I'll be there about seven,' I said. 'Now, do we have any results from your friends?'

'Yes, plenty. I just finished typing my email when you rang. I'll send it now and give you a chance to study what they all found out. Then we can discuss this as well, tonight.'

Two minutes later, my phone pinged; the email had arrived. Louise had itemised each friend's responses, which made interesting reading.

Hi Hugh.

Results below. They all rang different numbers. From their descriptions they were all answered by the same man.
Tim Rang 09:30 Labrador. Vaccinated. Ready now. £850
Terry. 09:50. Spaniel. With Mum. Chipped and Vaccinated. £900
Meryl. 10:30. Collie. 6 weeks old. Chipped. £600
Tony. 10:45. Boxer. With Mum. 7 weeks. Vaccinated. £1850
Corinne. 11:30 Miniature Poodle. 6 Weeks. Chipped. £1350
They could be seen at - guess where?- Hawthorn House, except one. Corinne was given a different address. She gave me the full address and post code. Appointments made for different days at either 10:30 or 15:30. Corinne was at 11.00 on Tuesday next. Cash only.

See you tonight.
Louise

If all these sales were to take place, someone would reap over £5000 for a morning's work. There would be nothing wrong in it if he treated the dogs properly, registered the operation with the Council and kept the kennels clean, but the lack of respect paid to the dogs and his avoidance of all the rules keeping the system clean meant that he needed to be stopped. Report him to the police? Or the Council? Or the RSPCA? But I was only finding out information for David, and there were other matters - people smuggling and money laundering – to be taken into account. And would Curtis Jandrell be held responsible for the deaths of twenty Koreans? A long spell at His Majesty's pleasure seemed to be in prospect. It would be up to David to decide on when to contact the authorities.

Twenty Three

Promptly at seven o'clock I walked up the path to Louise's conservatory.

Her bruising was wearing down to a pale green and yellow, not as noticeable as the day before. I settled into a sofa as she poured the drinks, then made herself comfortable in the other sofa.

Over a glass of wine, we commiserated over Tilly's death.

'Have you heard any more details during the day?' I asked.

'Yes,' she said. 'It was a foggy night and there have been no witnesses coming forward. Carter's Mill Road is a bit secluded and no dog walkers or joggers would have been out on a night like that.'

'How did she die' I asked.

'Her...her... throat had been cut.'

Louise had difficulty saying the words, so horrible was the thought of Tilly dying in that way. Tears began to roll down her cheeks as she explained that she had been crying off and on all afternoon.

I also felt the sadness. Although I had met Tilly only once, she had made a good impression because she did her best to tactfully protect me from the bouncers and helped me to find Louise. I had pictured her and Louise laughing together when they met on their shopping trip.

The doorbell rang.

A feeling of déja-vu passed through me. Another problem visitor? Louise was hesitant about going to the door but she went anyway. I vanished into the kitchen, as before, but hovered close to the hall door, listening, poised for trouble.

'Mrs Louise Sturgess?' The voice was familiar.

'Yes.'

'I'm Detective Inspector Natalie Thorpe and this is Detective Sergeant James Gilroy. May we come in and have a word?'

'Yes, of course. Come in,' Louise replied and led them into the lounge. 'I have a friend here. Will it be OK if he comes in with us?'

'Of course.'

I walked into the lounge and DI Thorpe turned and looked at me, quizzically, I thought. What ideas were running through her mind?

'Good evening, Mr Evans,' she said. 'We meet again.'

'Good evening to you,' I replied. I stayed non-committal.

'We met at Darren's shop, after the shooting,' I explained to Louise, who was obviously wondering how we could have known each other.

When we were all seated, DI Thorpe faced Louise.

'Would you tell me where you were last evening, please?'

'I was at Coco's with friends from 7.30 until 8.30, then returned home. I didn't go out again.'

'Was Mr Evans one of those friends?'

'We did have a brief chat while we were there, but he left at about eight o'clock.'

'And did anything happen after you came home?'

'Well, Mr Evans came round after nine to continue our chat.'

The inspector raised her eyebrows.

'Were there any other visitors?'

'Yes. I had a visit from a guy I used to work with.'

'What was his name?' asked James Gilroy, pen poised to write it down in his notebook.

'Gavin Scott.' A look passed between the officers.

'And what time did he leave?'

'Just before ten, I think.'

'Not here long, then?'

'No.'

'And what was the reason for his visit?'

'He brought a message from his boss. My ex-boss.'

'There seems to be a lot of background that I'm missing, here. Would you care to fill in the gaps in my knowledge, please?'

'It's quite simple. I worked at the Golden Rainbow Casino for years and I left after an altercation with Gavin. I then moved over to the Dragon's Lair. It seems that business at the Rainbow has dropped off. Lots of clients, footballers mostly, have moved across and Glen was blaming me.'

'Glen?' This from the sergeant, still scribbling furiously.

'Glen Dalby, the owner of the Rainbow. Gavin said that Glen blamed me and that I should stop harming his business or there may be repercussions.'

'He threatened you,' Natalie translated.

'You could say that.'

'Is that how you got those injuries?' She indicated Louise's face.

'No. That was something else.'

'What would you say was Gavin Scott's mood when he left you?'

'Not very happy.'

'That sounds like an understatement. Would you care to elaborate?'

Louise looked at me. I nodded my support.

'Gavin was a sex pest at the Rainbow. Quite a few women left because of him. I was one of them after he cornered me in the office and I had to fight him off to get away. Last night, he didn't know Mr Evans was in the kitchen. He thought I was alone and tried to take advantage of the situation, to carry on where he left off in the office, you might say, but Mr Evans intervened and pushed him out of the door. As I said, he was not very happy.'

'Perhaps, 'fuming and frustrated' might have been a better description?'

Louise smiled in reply, which DI Thorpe took as confirmation.

I decided to put a word in.

'Can I ask if your visit is in connection with anything in particular?'

'Of course. Last night, a lady was murdered in Carter's Mill Road and Mr Scott's name has been suggested as a suspect. I've questioned him and he mentioned you as his alibi. Hence my visit, to check it out. You've confirmed that he was here, but as he failed to get what he wanted here, he may have tried his luck elsewhere.'

'Poor Tilly.' Louise murmured.

'You knew the lady?' the detective said.

'Yes. We worked together at the Rainbow for years. It's very sad.'

'I agree.'

Then she looked at me.

'It's interesting to see you again, Mr Evans.'

'How so?' I asked.

'Two murders. Two bodies. And you turn up at both. I would call that very interesting.'

'Coincidence, I assure you.'

DI Thorpe glanced at our two wine glasses on the coffee table.

'So are you and Mrs Sturgess...friends?' she asked, unsure how to describe our relationship, but the emphasis suggested something more than a casual involvement.

'We have a mutual friend. He asked me to look up Mrs Sturgess while I was in Manchester. That's all.'

Natalie Thorpe assimilated this quietly, then said, 'Well, that will be all for now. We'll leave you to finish your wine. But I may need to talk to you again. Both of you.'

Louise heaved a big sigh of relief when the detectives left. She had had misgivings about speaking to them, misgivings that had proved unfounded as they were only checking on Gavin's alibi and their questions were not probing. Her replies had been short and to the point.

She reminded me of what Tilly had told her, that Gavin had said he would show Glen how to run his business. Following that, Darren had been killed and now Tilly. DI Thorpe had not mentioned whether there was any sign of a sexual attack. If so, Gavin would be firmly in the frame. If not, then perhaps he wasn't guilty. 'He had failed to get what he wanted here and decided to try his luck elsewhere' the inspector had said. Hopefully, forensics would show whether Tilly had been involved in any kind of a struggle.

We finally turned our attention to the email. After a brief perusal to refresh my memory about the puppy farm, I opened the conversation.

'All the calls were answered by the same man, they reported?'

'Yes. They all said he had a very distinctive voice. Gravelly, was the main description. So he must have a row of phones sitting there waiting for calls, each one for a particular breed,' Louise said.

'The viewing times are interesting. Well-spaced, to give time to drive up to Sperrymoor Farm to change breeds between viewings,' I noted.

'What is Hawthorn House like? Do they live there?' Louise asked.

'I don't think so. I looked in earlier. The kitchen was perfect. You could even say 'posh'. The lounge was a mess. Tatty furniture with a couple of throws to make it look respectable. I'd suspect that it's just a bit of comfort for the staff to sit between viewings, but I don't think they are there full time. One of the viewers told me that his wife had taken the little girl to the toilet and that was spotless, too. It strikes me that this is a show house; viewers only need to see the pups and they might need the toilet after a long drive, so that's what they get. I'd be surprised if anyone lived there. There was certainly no-one about when I arrived there earlier.'

I looked at the email again and went on.

'I'd suspect that none of the pups has been chipped or vaccinated. Saying they had been done on the phone was just lies; window-dressing; it impresses the customers and clinches the sale.'

We seem to have pieced together the picture of the operation. An advert with very little information, followed up by a phone call purporting to be to a different breeder; smart house in a remote situation; pleasant lady to do the selling; cash only; ker-ching!

'What does Bella look like?' I asked.

'Hal's wife?'

'Yes.'

'Early fifties. Been a looker in her time. Still dresses smartly. Why do you ask?'

'Ben Kealy, one of the buyers, mentioned that the lady at Hawthorn House was named Bella. Then you said that Hal's wife was Bella. She comes in carrying a shopping bag on Fridays, at the same time as Archie Moffatt. Is it too much of a coincidence to think that she is delivering the takings from the puppy enterprise?'

Louise agreed that it was a distinct possibility.

'If Friday morning is when the cash is collected together, we must ask ourselves: What happens to the money? There must be a large amount of cash to be banked each week,' she said.

'Have you noticed what happens after their Friday morning meeting? Does anyone go to the bank?' I asked.

'No. A security van calls at different times each week. There's a strongroom at the casino to keep the cash until they call. Curtis and Archie are the only ones who can open it. He's almost paranoid about it. I think Curtis would prefer it if he was the only one with a key, but the insurance company insisted on at least two keyholders. It didn't go down too well. He really doesn't trust anyone.'

We seemed to be getting into deep water. If Curtis had Archie Moffatt on board, there was no way that I could interfere.

'I think this is where the money laundering starts. I don't know enough about it to do anything about it. David will be the man to ask. I wouldn't be surprised if offshore accounts are involved. You know, Cayman Islands, Isle of Man, Singapore, Channel Islands, even Ireland, seem to be the ones we hear most about, but that's all I know.'

'I think it's a case of shuffling money about between accounts until it's not clear where it came from or where it's going to. No paper trail to follow,' Louise said.

'When you told me about the farm, you also mentioned a transport company amongst other businesses in this country. Any idea of the name?

'Denny Shaw's out at Failsworth.'

'That rings a bell,' I said, 'I've been there. It's beginning to fit together.'

'What is?'

'This jigsaw of money laundering. With a bit of false accounting.'

Louise filled our glasses again and made herself comfortable on the sofa,

'OK. Explain,' she said.

'I've only got a rough idea of how it works. We'll have to give David the facts and see if he can make sense of it all.

My phone buzzed. It was Bethan.

'Hello, Hugh. How are you?' she asked.

'Wonderful, as ever. How are you and Jess?'

'We're having a great time. Until I saw the news tonight.'

'Oh, what was it?'

'I was watching North West News on the telly and they mentioned a lot of violence in Manchester, including someone being murdered,'

'Oh, Tilly.'

'You knew her? I thought you were just going there to find out stuff for David. And now you're involved in all this violence!'

'Bethan, I promise, I'm not involved in any violence at all. Tilly was the receptionist at the first casino I went to and she told me where to find Louise. They worked together. They were friends. I only saw her the once. There's nothing to worry about. Honestly.'

'But it seems to me that you're dealing with some shady customers again. I do worry about you, you know.'

I reassured her once more and tried to change the subject. I asked her about her holiday. The change of scenery was a great benefit to her and we chatted until I had salved all her worries away and she was once more sounding like the Bethan that I loved. Happy again, she went back to cuddling Jess, though I secretly wished she wouldn't do that, and enjoying her holiday once more.

Louise was looking tired and I decided to leave.

'Before you go,' she began, 'I'd like to go and see Glen tomorrow. Perhaps I can clear the air about his threats. He always liked me, there are no hard feelings about my departure. Could you come with me, though? I'd feel much safer if you were there.'

'Of course I will.'

I thought hard for a moment or so.

'If I go there, say, half an hour before you, then if you are still being followed by Curtis's spies, they won't know that I'm with you on this. I'd prefer for Curtis not to know of my interest in his affairs.'

'Sounds like a good idea,' she said. 'The Rainbow opens at noon. I'll turn up at twelve-thirty. Meet you inside. I'll go straight from there to the Dragon's Lair, partly to show Curtis that I'm still not clear of the bruises, partly to defuse any thoughts he may have when my tail reports to him where I've been.'

I left the way I came. As I exited from Merlin Street, I could detect no car tailing me as I drove off into the night.

Twenty Four

It had been too late in the evening to ring David when I returned from Louise's. Instead, I had an early night and was up with the lark next morning. After a hearty full English breakfast, I reviewed all the information I had discovered so far, prior to ringing him next day. I wasn't due at the Golden Rainbow until twelve so there was ample time for me to speak to him. I just hoped that he wouldn't be travelling to Welshpool or Shrewsbury to deal with court cases.

Brenda West answered my call with her usual efficiency and put me through to David.

'You'll have to explain money laundering to me,' I began when the pleasantries were over. 'I can't quite grasp how it works. You mentioned off-shore bank accounts before. Where do they fit in? All I know about Curtis Jandrell is that he had a lot of money coming in from many sources. There's the casino, rents from properties, a puppy farm, Just Computers, I believe he also owns Denny Shaw's Truck Hire and the people smuggling. His accountant-adviser is Archie Moffatt and I don't know where to go to from here. On top of this, two people have been killed and Louise has been threatened as well as being struck by Curtis Jandrell. The bruising still hasn't gone down.'

David listened patiently to my call.

'You've found out more than I expected in a short time, Mr Evans. I'm impressed and very grateful. As regards the off-shore

129

accounts, there's nothing illegal in having an off-shore account. Anyone can open one. Hiding it is what makes it illegal. There are many reasons for having one. Their attractive interest rates or favourable tax treatment in the foreign country are the reasons why billionaires use them. Now with multiple companies that Curtis has, he moves money between the companies by way of loans and false invoices so that the money can finally come back to him legitimately. Then he buys something expensive, property perhaps, and away we go again, with even more money coming in from rents.'

'Right, it makes sense, now. And what if he's involved in the people smuggling?' I asked.

'I don't know why he would use this route. Perhaps he thinks that the authorities are so busy watching the short routes across the channel to the south coast that he feels they might be less vigilant on the long routes. Cherbourg to Rosslare is a nineteen- or twenty-hour journey. A long time for those poor people to be stuck in the back of a lorry, but then, he's not concerned with their welfare, just their money, which will probably have been paid into one of his off-shore accounts.'

David paused, whether it was for breath or to let me assimilate all this information wasn't clear. He went on.

'Curtis has a group of illegal immigrants to bring in from Ireland. He owns a computer company, quite legally, in Rosslare. He uses a delivery of computers from them to cover the journey, so about a hundred computers are stacked at the back of the container to hide the immigrants in front of it. The delivery note said there are seven hundred computers on board, so Border Force won't suspect anything as the container would be full and there would be no room for immigrants. The lorry should arrive back here and deliver the computers to Just Computers - another of Curtis's companies - and set the immigrants free to fend for themselves in Manchester. But this time it didn't arrive because it was caught up in the landslide. Is there any connection between Denny Shaw and Curtis?

'No,' I replied. 'The truck was hired over the phone by a caller who had hired before so Denny trusted him. The company name he used was Safe Delivery. There's nothing on the net under that name. Denny knew the driver of old and he always got paid in cash when the vehicle was returned. The police have interviewed Denny but got no further than the mystery caller. They've come to a dead end.'

This all seemed to make sense at last.

'The next step would seem to be reporting this to the police, or HMRC, then?' I said. 'The puppy farm to the Council or RSPCA?'

'Hold on,' David said. 'We don't have any proof that Curtis owns any of this. It's only your word against his at this stage. It would be like poking a stick into a wasp's nest to report what you've just told me and have him arrested. If we couldn't make it stick, Curtis's reaction would be worse than a nest of angry wasps. I don't want to get stung, thank you. We must spend a bit more time to find a connection that will stand up in court. Then we are more likely to be believed. You've got a few more days before Bethan returns home. Let's use them profitably.'

This wasn't the David I knew. Gone was the pleasant, calm, gentle David. Now he was commanding, dominating, not taking no for an answer. He knows what he wants and will make sure he's going to get it. What 'it' is I'm not sure, but for now, I would go along with him.

I had had my instructions. Time to get on with it.

131

Twenty Five

Just after twelve o'clock I walked into the Golden Rainbow Casino. Already there were players on the slot machines, hoping for a good start to the day. How long that would last would be as long a shot as betting on the Grand National. The Neanderthals were on duty early, the same two who distrusted my motives on the first visit, but there was no excuse to stop me entering now and I passed out of the foyer without hindrance. I thought I detected a look of 'Shall I, shan't I?' on one of their faces, but he decided in my favour and I was in.

I hung about close to the foyer, reading menus, posters, watching one of the many television screens showing loops of poker games and big wins on the roulette wheel to encourage the punters, as I killed time until Louise arrived.

She walked in dead on twelve thirty, said a cheery 'Hello' to the new receptionist. 'I'm here to see Glen,' she explained. 'I take it he's in?'

'Yes, he is,' was the reply.

'Thanks, Katy,' she said and turned to walk out of the foyer. The nearest Neanderthal, vastly overweight, with hair slicked back into a pony-tail and smelling of an overdose of cheap after-shave, stepped forward in her path.

'You're not welcome here, miss,'

'Hello, Reg. How's the wife and family?' Louise said, in her most disarming way.

'They're very well, thank you. And you're still not welcome here, miss.'

'Well, thanks for that. I'll tell Glen how efficient you are when I see him,' she said, flashing him a bright smile.

A tall man in a smart grey suit, pink shirt and yellow tie walked past me quickly and approached Louise.

She turned and saw him and smiled.

'Glen, how nice to see you. I was just telling Reg how efficient these boys are on the door. Could you spare me a few minutes to sort out a couple of things?'

'For you, anything. We'll go to my office.' He turned and led the way towards the 'Staff Only' door nearby.

'Can my friend come in with me, please?' she said, indicating me as I appeared in the doorway.

'Don't you trust me, then?' Glen smiled. 'Of course he can.'

He held out a hand in welcome. We exchanged names and shook hands. I don't think he noticed my lack of two fingers, as I have, over the years, perfected a handshake which camouflaged the deficiency.

We went down a corridor to a large room which resembled the flight deck of the star ship Enterprise. A bank of monitors blinked on one wall, showing CCTV images of all parts of the casino. Glen hadn't stinted himself when he designed this room. The large, wide desk contained a control deck which matched the monitor wall, with sliders and joysticks which would make a disc jockey the happiest man on the planet. Further back in the room stood a sofa and easy chairs around a walnut topped coffee table. This was served from a small kitchen area containing tea- and coffee-making paraphernalia with biscuits and marshmallows. On the other side of the room was a fully stocked bar and a couple of stools to match. Impressive,

We sat in the comfy area, as Glen called it as he offered us some refreshment, which we declined.

I was surprised to find him so civilised. He was suave, charming even, nothing like the rough-hewn gang leader I had been expecting. Obviously wealthy and smooth with it, but who would have expected him to be a drug dealer who had served time, who had henchmen like Gavin, who had possibly ordered the shooting of Darren?

'Well, Louise. What brings you here today?'

'I had an unwelcome visitor the other night...' she began.

'And who was that?' he asked.

'Gavin,' she replied.

'He didn't do that?' he said, indicating her bruises, looking shocked at the same time.

'No, no. That was someone else. But he did try it on again. Hugh stopped him and pushed him out of the door.'

Glen looked at me, admiringly.

'I'd like to have seen that,' he smiled, and I recalled Louise telling me that he had joked on the jail telephone about the stab wound she had inflicted on Gavin. I suspected that the two men didn't, perhaps, get on too well.

Louise went on.

'Gavin said you had sent him with a warning to stop poaching your customers, with dire threats of what would happen if I didn't stop it.'

'Oh, no!' He was clearly shocked. 'I didn't send him at all. And certainly not with that kind of a message. We were talking about the drop in takings and yes, you were mentioned. You've probably noticed yourself that some of our customers followed you to the Dragon's Lair, but that was to be expected. You were popular, attractive, great for business. They would have followed you if you'd gone to work for Tesco.'

'So you're not blaming me for your drop in takings?'

'No way. And I wouldn't threaten you with dire consequences, as you put it. You may come back to work here in the future, and you'd be welcomed with open arms.'

I would have liked to put a question about Darren's shooting, or Tilly, or David's wife Sallie's death, but this was not the time and the conversation was too interesting to interrupt, so I kept quiet. Glen went on.

'Gavin has this way of trying to show me how to run the business because he ran it when I was inside and he's wrong. I've only been out for a short time and I'm slowly finding out what he's been up to and I don't like it. He's developed a gang culture here. Yes, we're in competition with the Dragon's Lair, as with all the other casinos in town, and Curtis Jandrell has a different attitude to me. He seems to have a chip on his shoulder about something. I don't know what it is but it has made him more than competitive, he's vengeful. If there's any feuding going on, it's between Gavin and Curtis. Nothing to do with me.'

'I'm glad we've cleared the air,' Louise said. 'You never know, I may well come back to work here, but there would need to be a change of staff.'

'It's nice to hear it. I'll do what I can. I've already made changes. We now have a 'no drugs' policy. It seems to work for Curtis. It might bring a few punters back, you never know.'

'Poacher turned gamekeeper?' smiled Louise.

'Something like that.' He returned the smile.

We got to our feet and he ushered us through the door as we said our farewells. Back in the car, we both felt relieved. I was relieved that Glen seemed to be a reasonable kind of man and Gavin was the driving force of the tit-for-tat attacks. Louise was relieved to see her old boss in such good form. Twelve years in jail had not hardened him. He was not bitter. Or vengeful.

I drove across town to the Dragon's Lair.

'You can leave me here,' Louise said. 'I may be some time. I'll ring you later.'

I pulled up on the street. She got out of the car and walked towards the casino. A man came out of the door, heading for his car.

'Hi, Chaz. You OK?'

'Yes, fine, Lou' he said.

He got in, clipped his seat belt, turned the key and a loud explosion sent bits of his car flying into the air. There was no way in which he could have survived. Flames licked over the bodywork of the car and I could see Chaz in the front seat, with his head, bloodied from flying glass, lolling to one side. Was he already dead? In Falklands mode, I ran into the casino; Louise was already inside.

'Fire extinguishers!' I said.

She pointed to two on the wall next to the door. I grabbed one and ran out. I trained the jet on to the car and put out the flames on the driver's side. I opened the red-hot door and pulled Chaz out as best I could. My feelings were confirmed. He was dead. I laid him on the ground and directed the bouncer, who had followed me out with the other extinguisher, to work on the other side of the car. Between us we managed to prevent another explosion by keeping the fire away from the petrol tank.

Louise had run out to Chaz and confirmed that he had died. She used her coat to cover the body.

Within ten minutes the car park was a hive of activity. Passing rubber-neckers on the street, customers from the casino, office workers at their windows, all wanted to see the wreckage. Approaching sirens heralded the arrival of paramedics and fire crews to take charge of the situation.

'I'm going,' I said to Louise. 'There's nothing else I can do.'

I slipped into my car and drove away. I had no wish for publicity.

Twenty Six

I rang Detective Inspector Maldwyn Humphreys. He was pleased to hear from me and could up-date me on the immigrants' situation.

'I've received a report from the Home Office. I'll read from it for you. Forgive me if the language sounds a bit formal, but that's Whitehall for you, isn't it? Here goes.'

I could hear that he put his best news-reader's voice on to read the report.

'Post mortems were performed on site as the bodies were brought out. The inquest has been opened and adjourned and the bodies are released to the families. We can expect that the respective governments will bear the cost of transport to and from the airports, but not for the flight home. We have quotes from a couple of airlines for the transport of ashes and/or bodies and these are being transmitted to the families for them to decide. Cost may influence their decision as to whether or not to cremate. We await their replies.'

'Thanks for that,' I said, then continued 'so there will not be any funerals as we anticipated?'

'No. The bodies are in one of our temporary mortuaries at the moment. How long this will take depends on the speed in which we get a decision on final disposal from the families. This will be soon, I hope.'

'Be sure to let me know when they are to depart. I would like to see them off. I'm sure Grace would too.'

'You would be very welcome, after all you have done. Incidentally, Greater Manchester Police seem to have struck a brick wall in their investigations.'

I thought 'I could help them, but it's not my case, it's David's'.

I said, 'There's a lot going on up here, gangs wise. They'll have their hands full. I've only been here a week and I was present at a shooting and I was twenty yards away from a car bomb going off this afternoon. It's very busy.'

'There's something to be said for a rural patch, then,' he said.

We finished the call and I rang Grace's mobile.

Her quiet voice answered, barely audible above loud voices and kitchen sounds in the background.

'Hello, Grace. It's Hugh Evans.'

'Oh, Hugh. One moment. I'll go outside. It's quieter there.'

I heard her explaining that she had an important call to her boss, at least, that's what she told me she had done as it was in Korean.

'That's better,' she said. 'Fresh air as well. It's so hot in the kitchen. How are you, Hugh? It's been a while since we spoke.'

'I'm fine, thanks. I've been in Manchester for the last week. It's quite eventful. I'll tell you all about it when I see you. But I have heard from the police that the immigrants' bodies are to be sent to Korea soon, when the families have made a couple of decisions - whether to cremate or not, whether to bury them over here or not, whether they can afford repatriation or not.- you know how it is.'

'If it's a matter of money, I feel there's a lot of sympathy for them in this country. Perhaps we could try crowdfunding. That might help.'

'What a good idea!' I said. Why don't I think of things like that? I thought. 'I'll let you have an estimate of how much we'll need when I know it.'

'I'll set it up in the next couple of days...' I heard a door creak behind her and a stream of Korean flowed into - no, assailed - my ears from a voice which could only have been one person - her boss.

'I must go,' she said. 'Thank you, Hugh.'

The line went dead.

My next call was to David to bring him up to date with what was happening in Manchester. He was still in the office when Brenda put the call through. What a change from the clamour of an Asian kitchen to the peace of a rural solicitor's office.

'How are you, Hugh?' he began. 'Well, I hope?'

'Yes, thanks. It's all happening up here. The gang war is escalating. A couple of killings and a car bomb. I was close to the shooting and the bomb, too close.'

'But you're OK? I don't have to remind you to be careful,' David put in.

'So far, I've met Glen Dalby. He seemed OK. Smartly dressed; well spoken; likes Louise. He doesn't look like what I expected. Perhaps he's changed a lot while in prison. I'd be surprised if he did order Sallie's attack, as you suspect. Now Gavin Scott.- Red Rose Man, you remember?.- is a completely different kettle of fish. Hot headed, impulsive, vindictive and any other words you can think of along those lines. He wants to show his boss how to run his business. He could be the man who pulled the trigger.'

'That's very interesting,' David said. 'You've obviously got to know these people far better than I could have done from behind a desk. You are clearly the right man for the job, but be careful, you're getting too close to some of the bad things that are happening.'

140

'It's going to be difficult while I'm still working on the outside. I'll have to get more deeply involved if we're to find a solid connection between Curtis Jandrell and the Korean immigrants or the puppy farm.'

David replied, 'Exactly. If we can make those connections we can go to the police. If we go with just a few suspicions we could be regarded as cranks and time-wasters.'

Things are getting hotter.

I still had work to do.

Let's hope I can stay alive long enough to do it.

Twenty Seven

Louise rang me when she arrived home.

'How did it go with Curtis?' I asked.

'OK really. I told him that I was fed up with his spies watching me and to call it off.'

'What did he say to that?'

'He started with denying all knowledge of it, but he finally agreed it was over the top and called it off. Then he wanted to know your name. I told him you are a friend of a friend and that I'm showing you round Manchester during your visit here and really, your name is no business of his.'

'You told him to mind his own business? Brave girl!'

'Well, I had happened to mention that I could have him for assault. He didn't like that. He came out with the usual bluster. He said the bruises were wearing off now so nobody would believe me.'

'That's true. Pity we didn't take a photo when they were fresh.'

'No need,' she said. 'I told him I had been interviewed by the police the next night and they commented on the bruising. Or didn't his spies tell him the police had been round? They obviously had because he was very quiet after that. There were no further questions.'

'You'd got him on the run. Very clever.'

'He's expecting me back at work next week. Bruises or no bruises. He said that he's opening the new Mall in a couple of days, so he's busy with that; I could go to the opening as a guest, if I wanted to. I said I'd see and I left then. The police were looking for witnesses to the bombing. I gave them a statement. I said I had just arrived and met Chaz on his way to his car. I hadn't seen anyone near the car prior to that because I hadn't been there. I just said that someone had pulled him out of the car, didn't say who, relied on the fact that it was very confusing out there at the time. They understood. Curtis was very disturbed about it though. He's already plotting revenge.'

'You were lucky, though,' I said. 'Thirty seconds earlier you were walking past that car. You'd have been caught up in the blast.'

She shuddered.

'Don't remind me, Hugh. I was too busy to be scared when it happened, but now, when I think of what might have been, it makes me very scared indeed.'

We both needed some respite from an eventful day. We therefore agreed to meet for dinner at Coco's.

'I wonder if my secretary would like to book a booth for 7pm tonight?'

'Ah! Is that what they told you? I hadn't been sure what to say, so I said nothing. I could hardly say 'wife' or 'girlfriend', could I? That was their take on the call.'

'I wasn't complaining,' I laughed. 'I've never had a secretary before. I quite liked it. An upgrade to my status.'

We hung up. Louise was looking forward to a quiet afternoon. I had work to do.

Twenty Eight

'You've never had a chance to tell me about any other dodgy customers you've come across. That was the reason why David wanted me to contact you in the first place.'

Louise and I were back in Booth 3 at Coco's that evening. We sipped a couple of glasses of Pinot Grigio in the candle-light and I felt that the romantic atmosphere was likely to take over, though I didn't want it to; we had decided to eat out instead of meeting at her home for just that reason, to avoid getting too close. Having other people around would, hopefully, normalise the situation.

'One man comes to mind. Josh Redfern, a racehorse trainer,' said. 'The story goes that, in the past, he has served a two-year ban for doping horses, so he's open to a bit of smuggling. He has a small yard up in Lancashire and imports horses from Ireland. According to the gossip, he imports foreign workers as well, illegally, every time he comes from Ireland. A horse box with a couple of flighty yearlings in it is a good cover for a smuggler. He seems to get through without getting caught. He's often seen with Archie Moffatt at the casino, so I suspect he's taking advice from him as well.'

'It seems like the local pastime up here. It's not all happening on the south-east coast,' I said.

'No. The talk is that there's a network over the whole country, transferring illegals from one place to another. In addition to the new arrivals, there's the ones already here who are made to work for peanuts and accommodation, some who are hired out to farms or factories, some into prostitution and domestic service. Modern slavery is rife and a relatively small number of people are making fortunes out of it.

Louise was a mine of information on the subject. I supposed that she was so well-informed because of her job; hearing snippets here and there; bits of gossip; if you can keep your ears open you can learn all sorts of things. She told me that some of the customers will be spending big to get rid of ill-gotten gains and living the high life in the process. Spending big also provides an opportunity to win big, when it happens. As winnings are not taxable, it's a way of avoiding tax. Some will be at the casino in the hope of making new contacts. Louise was clever enough to piece together all these bits of information, though she was a long way from knowing the complete picture.

I told her about David's decision to delay reporting to anyone until we had positive proof of the connections. She agreed, though she expressed her reservations about me carrying on with my investigations on the grounds that things were getting dangerous and I was just an amateur in these things. The car bomb was still fresh in her mind. My reply of 'Don't you worry. I'll be OK' did nothing to reassure her.

We spent some time discussing my next move. Finding more about Josh Redfern would be a start. Tomorrow morning's assignment would be to find out where his yard was and make a visit. I would need a reason to call, and it couldn't be to look for a job, not at my age , with my scant knowledge of horses. Riding was one of the skills I had missed out on, along with getting a tune out of a violin and playing tennis. My grandfather's farm had gone over to tractors before I was old enough to help at harvest time , so I knew nothing about horses, and violins and tennis racquets were things the posh kids had for Christmas, not farm boys up in the hills.

Our thoughts were interrupted by my phone.

'Hello, Denny. You're working late,' I said.

'Well, you know what it's like. I'm a busy man.'

Yes, a busy man who is never too busy to chat, I thought.

'So, what does a busy man want this evening?' I asked.

'You know you were looking for a job? How are you fixed for a small job? Tomorrow. Just a trip in a van. Seventy-five quid. A hundred if you can get there and back in a day.'

'Where am I going?'

'Southampton.'

It sounded like a chance to find out more about the operation.

'OK. You're on.'

Josh Redfern would have to wait.

Twenty Nine

'I hope there's nothing illegal in this trip,' I had said when I picked up the van.

'Why d'you say that?'

'Well, You can't blame me for thinking why do we need a big van, going out empty.'

Denny was almost affronted that I had asked such a question.

He went on 'I wouldn't have anything to do with that line of business. I've got a customer who is rebuilding a 1953 Jowett Javelin and he's found a replacement engine online at Southampton. He needs it in a hurry, so don't hang about.'

'So that's why it's a big van. Sorry. I wasn't accusing you. You can't blame me for wondering these days' I said, getting into the Crafter's front seat. 'See you tonight.'

'It's over four hours each way, give or take. See you tonight.'

It was relaxed driving all the way down the motorways. I enjoyed a coffee break at the services. Sat nav helped me find the address in Southampton, which turned out to be on a trading estate. I looked for a sign for Jerry's Autos and found it tucked away in the back row of small lock-ups, between a sewing machine repairer and a picture-framer.

Jerry Wood was a cheerful fifty-ish man. He kept a very tidy repair shop. There were no cars waiting for attention outside, just one inside. He obviously was a specialist in his field, repairing classic cars to order, one at a time, no pressure.

After a cheerful welcome we decided to load the engine and then have a lunch break.

Loading the engine was no trouble; a portable hoist lifted it and put it into the van with very little effort on our part, the headroom in the Crafter making ample room for the hoist. I had imagined that we would have had to lift it in by hand, but Jerry was well organised and saved us the exertion.

I had purchased some wrapped pies and sandwiches at the motorway services, which made a passable lunch for me, with a mug of tea from Jerry's well-fitted but small kitchen area at the back of the lock-up.

I had a long journey ahead of me, so we cut our conversations short and I left.

I opened the door of the van and to my surprise I found a man sitting in the passenger seat. He was dark haired with a black beard, in fact everything about him was black, his jacket, his trousers, his shoes and his baseball cap.

'Hello, sir,' he said in a foreign accent. 'Are you able to take me to Birmingham, please? I have no money and I need to get back to my wife and child.' Perhaps I should have thrown him out there and then, but he was very polite, respectful even. So many thoughts went through my mind.

Hitch hiking isn't the safe operation it once was. There is so much wrongdoing these days that one thinks at least twice before picking up a stranger. And there is always the chance that he may not be in the country legally. The old 'what ifs' crowded into my mind.

What if he's spinning me a yarn?
What if I say no and it's true?
What if he's got a knife?
What if he steals the van?
What if he's an illegal?
What if we're stopped by the police?

I know everyone will say I made a mistake if it goes wrong, but his sincerity seemed genuine even at such a short acquaintance and I agreed to take him. Nagging doubts, though, made me check the back of the van. If this guy had got in without me hearing him, was he a decoy to cover a bunch of others slipping silently into the back? However, only the Jowett engine stood there, covered in a blanket; it was otherwise empty. We set off.

Afran was pleasant company. He told me he had lived in Birmingham for two years. He worked in a kebab shop in Smethwick and had been to Southampton to visit his brother who was in hospital. He was Kurdish, having left Iraq three years ago. He had arrived here on a government sponsored scheme, he assured me. He had experienced an amount of abuse from people who assumed that he was here illegally, so much so that he carried a knife for self-defence. As if to prove it he pulled it out of a long pocket in the lower leg of his trousers. My blood ran cold as I saw the most evil, insidious-looking knife I had ever seen.

'It's a smaller version of the Khanjar,' he explained, an element of pride in his voice. 'Back in history, they were made of steel with a sheath that was decorated with gold and jewels. It was made for close combat. The blade is curved, sharp on both edges with a pointed tip.' This description was said with relish, I thought. Was he looking forward to finding out how smoothly its double-edged blade would slip between ribs? Was I to find out how efficient a weapon it could be?

I was busy checking my mirrors to see what mayhem would be likely to occur if it was going to happen soon. Surely not while we were moving, but you never know.

'I hope I never have to use it,' he said as, to my relief, he slid it back into its sheath and zipped it into his pocket. 'My brother, Daryan, gave it to me. He is dying, and it belonged to our father. My brother passed it on to me. I will pass it on to my son when my

149

time comes. It will stay in the family as a reminder of our homeland.'

I felt reassured as the knife had been put away.

'I suppose you thought I was an illegal immigrant about to steal your van? he asked with a wry grin.

'I must confess, something like that had crossed my mind, but only when you showed me the knife. Actually, I'm quite sympathetic towards the immigrants. Of course there is a problem, but only of numbers. How can we process and accommodate the numbers that are arriving each day? There will be bad apples in every barrel, but the majority will be good apples. People who want to work and support their families in peace, which is something they cannot do in their homeland. They want to come here, desperately. Many of them die in the attempt. They have all my sympathy. Sorry, end of speech. I shouldn't go on like that.'

'No, it was a good speech. Thank you.'

We pulled into Frankley Services a short time later. I felt the need for a calming cup of tea. I had been in situations when death was one of the options many times in the Army, but so long ago that instinct had dimmed over the years, and I now needed time to consider my next move. A take-away mug of tea seemed the best option. We ended up with tea in cardboard cartons. As we stood in the car park, sipping the hot beverage, Afran expressed his appreciation of the journey.

'I am sorry that I frightened you with my knife,' he said. 'I noticed that you acted nervously when I showed it to you.'

'I must admit, you got me worried,' I said. 'It was interesting to see it, though. I'd never seen one close up before.'

'I would like to have seen an original one myself, decorated with jewels and with a poem engraved down the blade, a real work of art.'

We finished our tea, put the cups in the waste bin and Afran said, 'Thank you for the lift. I can find another lift from here, which will not delay your journey.'

We were approaching the van, and before I could reply, Afran rushed to the back doors. He had spotted two youths attempting to force the doors, no doubt thinking that we would be longer in the restaurant.

'Stop, now! he shouted.

They stopped what they were doing and ran away towards a bright yellow Mini parked nearby. Afran ran towards them, then, as the Mini roared away, turning towards the exit, it caught him a glancing blow which cannoned him into the side of our van. I ran to Afran who was rolling on the ground in agony. I dialled 999, calling for police and ambulance to attend.

As I laid my jacket over him, he whispered to me, 'My Khanjar; the police must not find it.'

I couldn't just go to his pocket as a small crowd was gathering. Seeing me with a knife would lead them to jump to all the wrong conclusions. It would be too incriminating to be seen with a knife.

I ran to the back of the van. Jerry Woods had lovingly laid a blanket over the precious engine. Now it became useful to protect Afran as he lay on the ground. I recovered my jacket and used it to conceal his dagger, which I managed to take out of his pocket under cover of the blanket. With jacket and dagger safely on the front seat, I turned my attention to the emergency crews which had arrived. They dispersed the small crowd of onlookers, having checked that none of them, surprisingly, had seen anything of what happened. The paramedics dealt with Afran, transferring him to the ambulance. The police constable, having established that I had been the only witness, took my name and address, then questioned me about what happened I told him what I knew.

'His name is Afran. He's Kurdish. Speaks good English. He works in a kebab shop in Smethwick and he has a wife and child.

A son, I think. I gave him a lift from Southampton where he was visiting his brother who is in hospital. That's all I know.'

'You don't know his surname?' he asked.

'No, and I don't think he knows my name either. Apart from the journey and a tea break we haven't had much time for full introductions.'

'Not many people give lifts to strangers these days. How are you so sure that he was genuine? Could he be here illegally, do you think?'

'Never entered my head,' I lied, but I didn't want to get involved in that discussion and have to divulge my thoughts when the dagger appeared.

'And what do you have in the van?'

'A car engine.'

'Don't be funny.'

'I'm not,' I said. I walked to the back of the van and opened the doors to reveal the Jowett engine.

'And where are you taking it to?' No apology for the misunderstanding, I noted.

'Manchester.'

'Why Manchester?'

'Because that's where I was engaged to do the trip. Denny Shaw Transport. Denny is the boss.'

'But your address is in…' he flicked back through his notebook 'in…(he avoided Llanynder)… Wales. How come? It's not making sense.'

'It's pretty straightforward to me. I live in Wales. My wife is on holiday in the Lake District. I decided to have a break in Manchester. I know it's not at the top of holiday destinations. Couple of matches to see. Look up an old friend. You know how it is. I'd met Denny Shaw and he said he was short of a driver to do a trip, picking up a special engine from Southampton for a customer of his. A 1953 Jowett Javelin. All his regular drivers are out. He's short-handed because one of them got killed the other week. He asked if I could help. So here I am, on my way back with the engine.'

There was nothing to say after that and he let me go, with a cautionary word that they may need to talk to me again, depending on how enquiries went.

The journey back to Manchester was mercifully uneventful and Denny was still on the yard when I arrived. After a relieved greeting, he went to the back doors of the van.

'What's happened here?' he asked, pointing to the scratch marks around the edge of the door.

'We stopped at Frankley and two youths attempted to break in. We chased them off before they got in.'

'We? Who's we?'

'I gave a lift to a chap from Southampton to Frankley. He ended up in hospital.'

'What?' Denny was panic stricken. He could see an insurance claim dancing before his eyes.

'I'd better explain this a bit better. Let's go into the office. The engine is OK, by the way. They didn't get in.'

With that reassurance, Denny calmed down and by the time I had told him the whole story, well, almost the whole story, he was satisfied that all was well with the van apart from the few scratches he had already seen.

I retrieved my jacket and Afran's Khanjar from the van, put them in my car and left.

I had thought that doing the trip would give me an insight into the people smuggling racket, but there had been no sign of anything illegal happening. On the other hand, Denny had said at the outset that he wouldn't have been involved in anything like that. His reaction to the thought of an insurance claim against him reassured me that he was too nervous to do anything dishonest.

There had been no point in telling Denny about the Khanjar. I would have to find a way of returning Afran's heirloom. A tour of all the kebab shops in Smethwick could be on the schedule.

I patted the notes in my pocket and drove off to the B&B.

Thirty

My slumbers that night were interspersed with a hooded silhouette of a man waving a full-sized Khanjar above my head like the sword of Damocles. A car load of Kurdish men passed through in a Jowett Javelin, as I sat on a hobby horse at a fairground and Denny Shaw presented me with a pile of twenty-pound notes as I passed him on each revolution of the roundabout. A bell was ringing in the distance and as I struggled through to the surface of consciousness, I realised that my phone was ringing in the real world. My efforts to awaken must have been obvious to the caller.

'Sorry if I've rung at the wrong time,' Detective Inspector Maldwyn Humphreys said. At least he didn't say 'Good afternoon' or 'It was a nice day when I got up' to rub in the fact that he had been up early and I hadn't. Those comments display the pride that early risers show in their so-called prowess. He didn't know that I had had a long day driving followed by a late night planning the course of the next few days. And a long telephone conversation with Bethan, who was having an enjoyable holiday with Jess and needed to tell me all about it.

'No, it's fine,' I said. He wouldn't have rung for anything trivial, therefore it must be important. So it was fine.

'I have news at last,' he said. 'We have received instructions from Korea. Fortunately, all of the immigrants are from the same

155

village, so contacting them is easy. Three of the families required a cremation for their relatives and the ashes returned to them; the other seventeen require the bodies to be sent home for burial. We will arrange to take them to the airport at this end and the South Korean Government will see to delivery at the other end. The cost of the flight home will be borne by the families. Cost wise, the ashes will be flown for £1500 each, bodies for £2000 each. That will add up to just under £40,000 for the families to find. They made a quick decision over disposal of the remains. Let's hope they can make another quick decision now.'

'I hope so. Grace, that's the lady who translated the letter, suggested crowdfunding. I'll ring her and see how she's getting on with it.' I said. 'Thanks for the update. I'll be in touch when I have some news.'

My alarm clock said it was just after nine. I hoped that Grace would not be starting work until later in the day and rang her mobile. It would be helpful for us to have a reasonable conversation without interruption by her boss, who seemed most unsympathetic to anything that was other than his business. She picked up on the third ring.

'Hello,' her quiet voice said.

'Hi, it's Hugh. Can we talk or are you at work?'

'I'm at home. We can talk. I'm not due in until ten-thirty.'

'I've just heard that the families have made their decision for repatriation. Three families have chosen cremations. The ashes, plus the other seventeen bodies will be returned to Korea as soon as possible. However, the cost is quite high, it adds up to almost forty-thousand-pounds. Have you had any luck with crowdfunding?'

'Just a little, about two-thousand-pounds so far, but it's only been open for a day or so. I have also been in touch with my parents in London. They know other Koreans in London - it's a kind of club - and they will be making a collection at the next

156

meeting. I think crowdfunding on the net will take some time. Is there a time limit for them to be repatriated?' she asked.

'Not sure, but I get the impression that they would like it done as soon as possible.'

'Can we give it a week and see what happens? Perhaps we'll have news from the families in Korea by then.'

'That sounds reasonable,' I said. 'I'll let Maldwyn Humphreys know. I'll be in touch soon.'

We ended the call, voluntarily this time, without instructions from her boss.

After a hectic start to the day, I could now get ready to do what I had planned – a visit to Josh Redfern's yard north of Preston.

I had missed the rush hour traffic. The twenty-or-so mile journey passed uneventfully and I arrived up on the moors to find a stone farmhouse flanked on one side by stone buildings which looked to be original, built of the same weathered stone at the same time and by the same pair of hands as the house. On the other side, a range of more modern concrete-block-built stables edged the yard, on which stood a shining new-looking horse-box in impressive blue and grey livery, with J REDFERN RACING emblazoned on the side in black lettering. The tailboard was down revealing the inside with its rubber floor and padded stall partitions, all designed for the comfort and safety of the horses. A young girl, teenager I reckoned, led a smart-looking horse, rugged-up for travelling, in a circuit around the yard as I got out of the car to watch over the stone wall which comprised the fourth side of the square.

'OK, Olga, lead him in,' a man's voice commanded from inside the nearest stable. The speaker emerged from the stable as Olga turned and the horse trotted up to the ramp and into the box.

'That was neatly done,' I said 'Are they all as good as that?'

The man looked up. He was about five-nine and wiry with it. His face was weather-beaten from a life spent outdoors, on these

moors presumably. The sleeves of his blue and white check shirt
were rolled up. Clearly, he had no need of protection from the cold
wind which blew across the moors around us. A gold tooth
sparkled as he spoke. He lifted the ramp and latched it closed, then
turned to me.

'Are you lost?' he asked.

'Yes and no, really,' I said.

'Well either you're lost or you're not lost, make your mind
up.'

'Yes, because I don't know where I am and no, because I'm
just driving round enjoying the countryside. I'll find my way back
to Manchester later on from wherever I end up.'

'That makes sense, I suppose,' was his grudging reply.

'It's just that I didn't expect to find racing stables up here. That
was a good-looking horse I saw just then. Is he racing today?' I felt
that I'd better show an interest, to get into conversation with him.

'Tomorrow. At Exeter. It's a two-day journey from up here.'

'I like racing, to watch, that is. I don't ride, unfortunately. My
mother would never let me have a pony when I was a kid.
Dangerous things, she reckoned. One end bites and the other end
kicks. So that was that. It was much later that I found that her fear
came from the fact that her twin sister was killed by a cart-horse
on their farm when she was eight. Mam never liked horses after
that.'

'Understandable, I suppose,' he said, though he had never been
afraid of horses and could barely understand Mam's fears.

'You're the boss here, are you?' I asked.

'Yes. Been here all my life.'

'It's a smart horse-box you've got, Mr Redfern.'

'Cost a fortune. But you have to have something good to travel
these horses about. Like today, for instance. Two days out and two
days back. There's accommodation for the groom and the driver. A

158

little kitchen. Otherwise you're stuck with bills for meals and B&B.'

It occurred to me that it was also useful for transferring illegals within UK, but I did not respond.

'Do you ever have Open Days?' I asked.

'No. That's for the big trainers down south. Famous names. Celebrities, you might say. We're not even near a village and I only have a few horses in. I'm not famous, just a hard-working trainer. So there's no Open Days for me. I can show you round, though, if you're interested.'

'I'd like to have a look, thanks.'

I drove my car off the road into his yard and parked. My first impression was of a very tidy yard. Not a weed; not a wisp of hay; no leaves in corners; no straw blowing in the wind. Despite their age, the buildings looked solid – no tumbledown buildings here - with doors and window frames freshly painted. The doors of the stone buildings were all padlocked and the windows boarded up.

'You don't have horses in those?' I asked.

'No. Used for storage most of the time or a few sheep now and again. Kind of a hospital as well, if something gets injured and needs treatment,' he explained. These buildings were not part of the tour.

We headed into the modern construction across the yard. Inside, the buildings were clean and modern. A wide corridor ran along the whole length of the building across the front of a row of five stables. As we walked along the row, inquisitive horses' heads appeared over the doors snickering in greeting. In the tack room, again neat and clean, Josh pointed out the various items of horse clothing, from bits and bridles to boots and bandages, which the horses wore for protection while travelling. I recognised what the smart horse I saw earlier was wearing for the journey to Exeter. However, felt boots for air travel were something I would never have thought of.

159

Olga sat cleaning some leather straps in the tack room, and as Josh was called to the house to take a phone call, I took the opportunity to speak to her.

'Do you enjoy working with horses?' I asked. A fairly obvious question to ask, but would do for an opener.

'It's OK,' she answered. Her eyes were flicking towards the door as though she was expecting Josh to come back and find her chatting. I detected an accent, despite the brevity of her reply.

'Where are you from?'

'Croatia.'

'Dobre jutro,' I said, hoping the few words of Croatian learnt on a holiday in Dubrovnik in the nineties would bring a smile to her face, but there was no response whatever. Perhaps she wasn't having a good morning.

'Have you been here long?'

'Six months.' A fearful look crossed her face. 'Are you police?' she asked. So that was the cause of her reticence.

'No, not police.'

'You must not tell anyone I am here,' she said, panic in her eyes.

'Do you live here?'

'Yes. I do not go off the farm.'

'How old are you, Olga?'

'Fourteen…'

The sound of approaching boots on the concrete path outside cut her off. Her head went down to continue the polishing. End of conversation.

'Sorry about that. Man in Ireland with a horse to sell. Couldn't get him off the phone,' Josh said as he came in.

I moved towards the door, nodding towards Olga as I went.

'We'd better leave her to it. Seems very keen on her work. I couldn't get a word out of her.' I said, forestalling any possible retribution he might mete out for speaking to strangers.

160

'Yes, she's not very chatty.' Josh replied with, I thought, a touch of relief in his voice.

Out on the yard, our tour came to an end.

'That was very interesting. Thank you for showing me round. What's the name of the horse that's going to Exeter?'

'Buccaneer. Why?'

'I might have a bet tomorrow.'

'I'm not sending him that far away to come back empty-handed. Could be a good each-way bet.'

I got into my car and drove on up the moors, then found my way on to the M6 and was back in Manchester in time for lunch.

Thirty One

Greg Dalby was lying motionless in his hospital bed. Festoons of tubes and wires were keeping him alive, bringing pings and bleeps from the machines near the bed. As long as they bleeped and pinged there was hope that he would survive. His pale face showed some heavy bruising, caused, they said, by the air-bag as it exploded before him. A skull-cap of bandages covered what was reported as a nasty gash on his head. The radiologist had told us that he had broken ribs, his right leg was fractured as was his right arm. His seat belt had broken his collar-bone, so violent was the sudden stop. Of more concern was the fact that he had been unconscious for a day and a half the night. By afternoon he was just about able to chat.

When I had returned from my trip to Josh Redfern's yard, I took my lunch at a café in Stockport. Stylish and neat, it offered a nutritious lunch at a reasonable price. It's surprising how prices go down the further away one was from the city centre. My second cup of tea was interrupted by my mobile buzzing in my pocket. It was Louise.

'Hugh. It's me, Louise. I've just heard that Glen has been in a crash and is in hospital.'

'How is he?' I asked.

'All they've said is that he's unconscious and has multiple injuries. I've spoken to the hospital and they say that it's not worth going in to see him today; leave it until tomorrow as they're dealing with all his injuries today. It must be bad.'

'Did they say how it happened?'

'Head on crash, they said. They had no other details.'

'Who would be able to tell us where it happened?'

Louise thought for a moment.

'I'll ring Katy, the new receptionist at the Rainbow. She might know. I'll ring you back.' She hung up.

I finished my now cold cup of tea, paid up and left.

I was sitting in my car when the phone rang again.

'Katy says that Glen ran into a lorry on the way to a meeting in Rochdale,' Louise reported. 'Due to the extent of his injuries, no one can go to see him until tomorrow at the earliest.'

It was therefore the next afternoon when we eventually stood by his bed. Louise was most concerned about her old employer's welfare. His estranged wife, who had left him when his drug crimes and incarceration had proved too much for her, was not interested enough to visit. She hadn't even asked Louise for updates on his progress. 'He probably asked for it,' had been her unsympathetic comment before pressing the red button on her mobile and finishing the call abruptly.

It was a very groggy Glen who had regained consciousness during the night. He was unable to recall anything about the accident, other than the side of the lorry filling his windscreen before the impact. His speech was slow and he seemed pleased that Louise had come to see him that afternoon. Nobody else had.

A glow from a high-vis jacket on the frosted glass of the door heralded the arrival of a police constable.

'How is he?' he asked Louise.

'Groggy, but talking. He says he remembers very little about the crash, just that he ran into a lorry on his way to Rochdale.'

'That's a start, then. I'll need to ask him a few questions, as he's up to it. The doctor said it's OK.' He addressed Glen. 'Good

163

afternoon, Mr Dalby. I'll try to be brief. You'll be tired after this ordeal. Can you take me through what happened?'

Glen struggled to recall the event. 'I was driving to Rochdale and a lorry pulled out of a road in front of me. I hit the brakes but it was too late. After that, nothing till I woke up here this morning.'

'Had you had a drink before going out?'

Glen smiled as best he could, the kind of smile that says 'What a stupid question,' but he replied civilly.

'No. It was nine thirty when I left the casino. Too early for alcohol, I'm afraid.'

'What about drugs?'

'Ah, you've been looking at my record, then. I was a drug dealer. I have never taken drugs. I did my time. And I don't deal drugs any more. So no, I wasn't high on drugs.'

Irritation was starting to show and the constable decided to change tack; he didn't want to antagonise a sick man; that would be entirely unproductive.

'Did you have the radio on. Could you have been changing stations, looking at the controls?' Glen's eyes rolled in tired exasperation.

'Take your time. No rush.' The constable was careful not to press too hard.

'No. I don't usually have the radio on. It's only pop and prattle at that time of the day. Morons ringing up about potholes, or the government, or the price of cheese.'

'Can you remember whether there was a name on the side of the lorry? It might have registered just before you hit.'

'No. Nothing. Is there anything on the dash-cam?'

'Well, we've looked at the footage on the dash-cam, Mr Dalby and it's very informative, up to a point. It shows you travelling at a reasonable speed and the lorry waiting to come out from a side road on the right. At the last second the lorry starts to move

164

forward into your path. There is no name on the lorry, either on the side or on the door. We can see the lorry moving forward, fast. Then nothing. It stopped recording. Lack of power as the front of your car was shattered by the impact, no doubt. The vehicle examiners told me that the lorry's hand-brake was on, so it had stopped in front of you. This makes it deliberate. Is there anyone who would want revenge for something you've done or not done?'

Glen flashed a look at Louise. 'Nobody I can think of,' he said.

The constable went on.

'One last question. You have a casino. Is there anyone who could be a disgruntled customer? Someone who thinks he won but you're not paying out. Or thinks the roulette table is rigged when he loses.'

'No. Nothing like that.' He obviously didn't want to say too much to the police, but his mind, and Louise's, and mine, went to Curtis Jandrell, but he would take whatever retribution was necessary without police assistance, or, as he saw it, interference.

The constable put his pencil and pad away.

'Why did you ask me if I saw a name on the lorry if you had already checked the dash-cam?' Glen asked.

'Just to see how your memory is, sir. It could have prompted other memories, too, such as seeing whoever got out of the lorry as it moved forward.'

'Well, I didn't see anyone.' Glen was getting tired.

'Have you traced the lorry. Who owns it?' I asked.

'We traced it from the number plate. It was owned by a firm in Rochdale. J R Newkirk and Sons.'

'Never heard of them,' came from the bed.

'It was reported stolen last night. Obviously, someone had planned this. It wasn't a road traffic accident. It was attempted murder.'

Letting this hang in the air, the constable departed.

'Has he gone?' Glen asked.

I stepped into the corridor and checked in both directions. There was no yellow glow in either.

'Yes,' I said.

'This was Jandrell's doing. Gavin's trying to stoke up this war and we're suffering. First Tilly, now me. With my record, I can't afford to get involved. I'm on licence. If I drop litter I expect to be sent back inside. It's got to stop, but I don't know how to stop it without confrontation. All-out war will do nobody any good.' The effort had tired him out. It was time to leave.

I said nothing. However, I thought a lot. If all my investigations came to fruition, the downfall of Curtis Jandrell was assured, leaving the field clear for Glen Dalby to prosper. I could not tell him that at this stage, though.

Thirty Two

We sat in Louise's lounge, just the two of us. Glen's crash had hit Louise hard. Of all the knocks she had experienced through life, seeing Glen in hospital was up there with the hardest. It was also close to home. Her present employer could not hold a candle to her first. She had only left the Golden Rainbow to avoid Gavin's unwanted attentions. She had always got on well with Glen, even when he was inside; their occasional phone calls were always amicable, and she had looked forward to his release. Where Glen was kind and reasonable, Curtis was wild and overbearing - and violent, as she had discovered. We went through the pros and cons of her employers. Glen came out on top in every comparison, but she could not go back to the Rainbow while Gavin was there. She was equally reluctant to return to work at the Dragon's Lair, where contact with Curtis was unavoidable, and she had no desire to repeat the treatment meted out during their previous violent encounter. Perhaps a move to different employment altogether would be better; at least she would be away from the war that was building up between the casinos.

So far, the tit-for-tat attacks had followed a pattern. First was Darren, the electronics expert, an important cog in Curtis's machine. Curtis hit back with Tilly, so cruelly murdered one dark, foggy night. Gavin then gets audacious, blowing up Chaz; on Curtis's forecourt, if you please. Finally, Glen is hit by a lorry and ends up in hospital. The thought that Louise could be next on Gavin's hit list sent shivers down both our spines.

For my own part, I could see myself being dragged into this gang war. I had come here to find information for David, but, inexorably, bit by bit, I was becoming involved in the conflict. Protecting Louise was now a priority, as were revealing Curtis's wrong-doings and Gavin's crimes. Rehoming the dogs at Sperrymoor Farm came close, with finding out what really happened to David's poor wife, Sallie, following on behind.

Over and above everything else, I felt a need to avenge the deaths of those immigrants, who died so miserably in my homeland. The landslide, of course, was nobody's fault, but it was the greed of the callous money-grabbers which had put them in its way in the first place. And as DI Thorpe had observed, death seemed to follow me every step of the way. The thought that I could pack up my bags and return to Llanynder, leaving them all to it, was a complete non-starter.

Our thoughts turned to what we could do to find evidence of Curtis's money-laundering. The Friday morning meeting was where the decisions were made, but there was no way in which we could eavesdrop on that.

Louise said, 'It's like Fort Knox, it's so secret. Hal in the corridor sees to that. You've seen him at work. The only people allowed in on a Friday morning are Bella with her shopping bag and Jimmy Quayle.'

'Jimmy Quayle? Who's Jimmy Quayle?' I asked. 'Handyman? Cleaner's assistant? Window Cleaner?'

'None of those,' she laughed, 'He's an office boy. He always goes in later than everyone else and leaves with a holdall about ten minutes after. I don't know what's in it.'

'Any idea where he goes from there?'

'Not really. His mother lives on the Isle of Man and he goes home to see her every week. The rest of the time he's in the office, so I rarely see him. Very devoted to his mum, so they say.'

'They?'

'The rest of the staff. Some of them call him Mummy's Boy. Bit cruel, really. You know what some people are like with nick names.'

'Yes, true enough. And the hold-all?'

'That goes with him to the Isle of Man. It must be something for his mother.'

'What would Curtis be sending to Mrs Quayle, I wonder?' I did my wondering out loud.

'I know Jimmy takes his week's washing home for his mother to deal with. I've commented once or twice about his bright white shirt at work. He's always very smart. He usually replies with 'You must thank me mother. She does it.' That's all I know about him.'

'What's in the holdall, I wonder. The only way I'll find out is to follow him to see where he goes and what he does. I'd suggest you came with me, but he knows you, so that would blow our cover straight away. I'll have to go alone. How does he travel?'

'He gets a taxi from the casino, but I've heard he sometimes uses the ferry from Heysham or Liverpool and sometimes he flies from Manchester or Liverpool. Rarely the same one twice in succession. I don't know why that is. It might be price or time of day or the departure time, I'm not sure.'

'I've been thinking about Bella's shopping bag. If it's not holding cleaning materials, what else could it hold? It can't be her private shopping, she would leave it in the corridor with Hal or in the staff room rather than take it into what sounds like an important meeting every Friday. But as she is also the seller of the pups, it could well be the week's takings from puppy sales.'

'Would that be much?' Louise asked.

'I've spent some time doing a few calculations and I'm amazed at how the sums worked out. The size of the building at Sperrymoor Farm would hold at least ten bitches. Average litter size would be about six. That's sixty pups. Two litters a year equals a hundred and twenty pups. Looking through the adverts, the average price seems to be eight hundred pounds, from two hundred for a Border Collie (some farmers are more realistic with their pricing) to over two thousand pounds for Boxers and French Bulldogs. My calculator showed that the total annual income would be almost a hundred thousand pounds! Small dogs, such as Toy Poodles and Yorkshire Terriers, would command even higher prices, but no doubt the smaller litter size would bring in less than a normal litter from a bigger, more robust breed. Somebody is making a small fortune out of those poor dogs. Added to which, it's all in cash.

'Why do you say that?' she said.

'Because the sales are all done as though it's a private seller and private sellers don't usually have card machines.'

'Of course,' she said, 'and it's got to be got rid of.'

A plan was formulating in my mind.

Next morning, I was sitting outside the Dragon's Lair, observing the comings and goings. At ten o'clock, a taxi drove into the forecourt of the casino. A lady got out, a smart lady, carrying a bulging shopping bag. She walked confidently up the steps and into the casino, bidding 'Good Morning' to the staff she met on the way. 'That must be Bella,' I decided.

Sure enough, twenty minutes later, a young man carrying a holdall emerged. As if by magic, a taxi arrived, he got in and it drove away. No directions were given to the driver. No doubt, they would be supplied inside the car or had been given at the time of booking. Fortunately, I had parked facing the correct direction to follow it so I did so, at a distance, identifying the taxi from the advert for a recently released Tom Hanks film emblazoned on the back.

The destination turned out to be Liverpool Pier Head, where the *Manannan* was waiting.

I made my way into the ticket office and purchased a return ticket. I expected to return on the next day if possible, or later if necessary. I wasn't sure what Jimmy would be doing, but time would tell. I would be ready, whatever he did.

The crossing on the *Manannan* was swift and smooth. The barman at the well-stocked bar told me it was always swift, just over two hours-it had been nearly four before this catamaran had arrived-but it was not always smooth-the Irish Sea was noted for being rough. I had never experienced this trip; my information was only hearsay, so I found that the barman was a mine of information about the company. He told me that way back in the days of sail, when the company was formed, ships could be held up at sea for days, unable to complete the journey because of high winds. That made two-and -a-quarter hours seem speedy, though it would be a pleasure to spend more time aboard this ship, with its two cinema lounges, a large bar and café.

I disembarked at Douglas, keeping Jimmy Quayle in view. I hung back, allowing him to get ahead of me. Passengers dispersed, some into waiting taxis or relatives' cars; one or two made for the nearby bus stop and others hurried on foot in different directions from the impressive, curved frontage of the terminal building, vanishing into the busy town ahead.

Jimmy was in this latter group. All through the journey he had sat in his seat, constantly checking that his holdall was still by his side, checking more often than the security of his week's washing would warrant, I felt. Once he was ashore, he made a bee-line for his destination, looking frequently at his watch. Into Athol Street, then down a side street and into Nico's Launderette. I strolled past, pausing for a moment or two to read the price list taped to the window. Inside, Jimmy was taking a laundry bag out of his holdall and giving it to an assistant in an overall with 'Nico's' embroidered on the breast pocket. As she moved towards the next empty machine, Jimmy picked up his holdall and came to the door. I walked on, not wishing to make any contact, even eye contact, with Jimmy as he left, calling back to the assistant as he did so.

'I'll pick it up tomorrow, as usual. Thanks Mum.'

He turned away and made his way back into Athol Street. I followed slowly, there was no crowd for me to merge into for cover. There were some imposing buildings here. Small Georgian panes in the windows, no garish advertising, a barber shop with just a red and white pole to advertise its existence, the street reeked of class. Even discreet brass plates were absent. Some of the buildings were residential, others commercial. The only announcement of their existence was perhaps a small sticker in a window or a barely visible board bearing a logo and a couple of initials of the company name.

So busy was I, taking in the new city scene, that I almost missed seeing Jimmy turning into one of the doorways. When I was closer, I could read the sign CWM with the words CAYMAN WEALTH MANAGEMENT in small letters beneath it, one of the many banks in Douglas. I followed him into the foyer. Ahead of me was a receptionist seated at her desk. To her left was a security door of reinforced glass, leading to a comfortably furnished area with low tables and armchairs where cashiers attended to their customers' needs. Much different from the banks at home, but then, this was a bank for the seriously wealthy. I asked the receptionist about the procedure for opening an account and she picked a prospectus out of an adjacent rack. I could see Jimmy through the glass door, sitting at a table taking a large amount of cash out of the holdall for the cashier to count it.

This has to be the takings from a week of selling puppies, no doubt topped up with surplus from the casino or rents, as advised by Archie Moffatt. It passed into the welcoming hands of an off-shore account, waiting for Archie to perform his wizardry to make it vanish and reappear as legitimate money.

I had settled on a small settee to read my prospectus and waited until Jimmy came out. The receptionist looked up and smiled.

'All complete?' she asked him.

'Yes. All done, Beverley.'

'Give my regards to Mr Jandrell,' she said as Jimmy walked to the door.

In a short time since we arrived in Douglas, Jimmy had answered both the questions which were unanswered when we left Liverpool. Was he really taking his washing to his mother? Yes. Was he bringing money on to the island? Yes.

Mission accomplished, I walked on and was surprised that at the end of the street I could see green hills rising ahead. This city centre of high finance, these imposing buildings, all stood in pleasant green countryside, a reminder of home. Perhaps I had spent too long in Manchester. I made a mental note to bring Bethan here for a holiday; she would enjoy it, I was sure. So would Jess.

Thirty Three

What Darren had called a 'precinct' turned out to be a very smart shopping mall. What had been a hastily erected office block in the 50's on the site of a bombed-out nineteenth century mill had been eventually demolished by Curtis Jandrell and replaced by an imposing building. He and his designer certainly had a great sense of style if the Hinton Court Mall and the Dragon's Lair were anything to go by.

The crowds had gathered early to be first to benefit from the bargains that would be on offer on opening day. All the shops had been rented, some well-known High Street names added to its status, along with some locally well-known Manchester traders. Clever lighting and shiny floors brought sparkle to the occasion. The Marston Mill Brass Band filled the echoing halls with music. Marches, songs from the shows and pop songs were designed to bring people in from outside, even if only out of curiosity to see what it was all about.

Temporary barriers blocked the entrance hall, leaving an area just inside the doors for the spectators to congregate for the grand opening. At least they would be under cover if it happened to rain. Behind the barriers, a bright yellow ribbon crossed the full width of the hall, ready for the formal opening.

In front of the barriers and behind the yellow ribbon, I could see Curtis with a few of his employees, including Louise, with the Master of Ceremonies for the day.

174

The band paused for Robin Banks, (not his real name, I suspect) a popular DJ from Northwest Radio, to pick up the microphone and welcome the crowd, generating a real carnival atmosphere into the proceedings.

'Good morning, everybody!' he shouted.

'Good morning, Robin!' they yelled, entering into the spirit.

'What a wonderful addition to this part of Manchester. No need to go up to town. Here on our doorstep, all these shops. High Street names. Local names. I see Albie's here with his pies. Keep one for me Albie!'

A thumbs-up came from a rotund gentleman in a traditional butcher's apron standing in a pie-shop doorway, who then patted his ample paunch as an advert for his tasty pies.

'Good old Albie!' came from a voice at the back.

Robin pressed on, introducing all the local shopkeepers by name with a complimentary quip about each. The crowd loved it.

'And now, with thanks to Mr Curtis Jandrell of the Dragon's Lair, whose foresight, and money, (laughter from the crowd) have made this possible…' Curtis, wearing his hoodie, waved from the background.

'Speech! Speech!' a couple of voices called out.

Curtis waved and melted into a shop doorway behind him. He was not one for publicity.

'So it is my great pleasure…' Robin continued, his speech punctuated by cheers, 'to hand this pair of golden scissors to a man who has scored goals for United, (hurrah) he's scored goals for England, (hurrah) the one and onlyyyy …Kelvin Antonio.'

The cheers were tumultuous.

'Kelvin will now cut the ribbon.' His words were lost in the din.

Kelvin took the mike and said, 'I declare this shopping mall open!' and with a flourish, cut the ribbon.

The crowd surged forward as Robin and Kelvin took cover in an adjacent shop and Curtis's yellow-coated men removed the barriers.

I had stayed at the back of the crowd, near the door, so that I could make a quick exit when the ceremony was over. Today was not the day to pay a visit to Just Computers, if it had ever moved here now that Darren was gone.

As the people moved forward, I noticed one or two characters that I would not have expected to see in this crowd. Burly men, all in black, pushing old ladies aside to get to the front. Then it wasn't one or two; it was three or four, no, six or eight.

Curtis's heavies had noticed them too and moved forward to head them off. All of a sudden, blows were struck, a fight developed, among screams from the many women caught up in the melee. A young constable put his head in through the door and decided at a glance that reinforcements were needed and was immediately in touch with his colleagues. Meanwhile, the tables outside the Cosy Café were overturned and the chairs used as weapons. The sound of men shouting, women screaming, a window shattered by a metal chair, pot plants tipped over, filled the air.

I helped some of the fallen customers to their feet and to take refuge in the nearest shops. Sirens heralded the arrival of the police, who rushed in and took control. I discreetly slipped out of the door just in time to see Gavin making for his car. This was no spontaneous fight. The men in black had obviously been orchestrated to spoil Curtis's big day and to wreak as much damage to the Mall, both to the building and to its reputation, as possible.

Gavin clearly wished to avoid the police questions. He had only come along to marshal his men before the fight and left before he could be identified as the instigator of it. Tit for tat continues, it seems.

176

Thirty Four

I treated myself to a mid-morning coffee after the earlier excitement. My phone buzzed.

'Hello,' I said.

'Hello, Hugh. It's Grace. I have good news. I have raised two thousand pounds by crowd-funding and guess what?'

'What? You tell me.'

'We have the rest of the money as well.'

'That's wonderful! How come?'

'I told you that my parents go to a Korean club. Well, one of the members is Mr Park Jong-yop.'

'Doesn't ring any bells. Who is he?'

'He's the owner of an electronics company in Surrey. He's a millionaire twice over. He will donate as much as we need to get those poor people home. He said he would like to come to see them off on the plane, as well.'

She was clearly overjoyed at the news of this success. Bubbly would be a better description.

'That's brilliant news,' I said. 'I'll ring Maldwyn Humphreys and get things moving. I'll keep you informed of the date and time. Well done, Grace. You've done well.'

We hung up and I rang Maldwyn Humphreys straight away.

'Hello, Mr Evans,' he said. 'What news do you have for me today?'

'Only good news today. We have the money. A Korean industrialist is paying for his countrymen to be repatriated. So you can start the ball rolling. If you can let me know date and time and which airport, I can set it up at our end. Both Grace and our benefactor would like to join me there to see them off. As it's going to be a cargo flight, can you make sure that we will be allowed into the freight area, please? That would be a great favour.'

'I'll do it gladly,' Maldwyn said. 'I also have good news. The cremations have been done and the ashes stored, so everything is ready to go. It's just a matter of making arrangements now. Leave it with me. I'll be back to you soon.'

He would have plenty to do - contacting the Home Office to arrange the flight and airport passes, Border Force regarding the immigrants, the Korean Embassy to notify the families - the list seemed endless.

Finding the lorry had certainly widened his experience.

Thirty Five

Next morning I went round to Louise's house once again. There was no need to avoid Curtis's spies on this occasion. I was interested to hear of Curtis's reaction to the fracas at the Mall. Over a cup of coffee from her machine, Louise told me that he had taken it badly.

'We had a kind of staff meeting. Jimmy was there and Hal and Bella. He blamed everyone for the attack. He's sure it came from the Rainbow. I took my life in my hands when I pointed out that Glen was in hospital, too ill to organise something like that.

'It doesn't stop him issuing orders, does it?' he said, 'and who gave you the right to speak on his behalf?'

Louise went on. 'I thought he was going to hit me again, but he was too far away, across a table, or he might have done. I didn't answer. I just dropped out of the conversation.'

'So who else did he blame?' I asked.

'He blamed Jimmy Quayle for not employing a stronger security force from the agency; the agency was at fault for not having enough staff trained in unarmed combat, as he called it. He blamed the police for a measly single officer on duty, even though that was what he had asked for, expecting no crowd control problems from the old dears and young mums who would be the likely customers. Half a dozen men in yellow coats would be sufficient to direct customers to wherever they wanted to go, particularly as the toilets and baby changing rooms were well signposted. All in all, he blamed everyone except himself.'

'What could he be blamed for, then?' I asked.

'Jimmy asked him where the Chuckle Brothers were.' she replied.

'The Chuckle Brothers? Who are they?' I was mystified at the new names.

'They're two Nigerian wrestlers. Big fellows. Evil looking men. Slit your throat for looking at them the wrong way if they felt like it. They're his special bouncers. People like Reg at the Rainbow or Hal here are ok for door keeping, but these two come into play if a customer needs to be threatened. I think their name is Chukwu or something like that, Obi and Dola, but nobody uses those names, in fact, nobody on the staff speaks to them as a rule.'

'Did Jimmy get an answer to his question?'

'Yes. He was told to mind his own business. Apparently, they were away doing a special job for him, or so he said. Then Jimmy carried on. I tried to shush him up but he insisted.

'Was it that urgent?' he asked. Curtis hit the roof.

'It's not up to you to query my decisions.'

Jimmy came back with 'You're blaming me for the lack of security men when you're sending your own men away - to do something underhand, no doubt. It's not fair.'

'I'll show you what's fair. Nobody tells me what's fair,' Curtis shouted and thumped the table, then left it at that. He didn't hit him or throw him out of the room, but he'll never forget it either. The meeting broke up with Curtis saying that he would see some of us tomorrow. We couldn't work out what that meant, but nobody dared ask.'

'Funny thing to say. Is someone going to be sacked.' I said.

She continued, 'When we were outside, we all wondered what he meant and sacking was all we could think of. Perhaps he'll cool down by tomorrow. Hal and Bella were going in to work this afternoon, but Jimmy and I are not in until tomorrow.'

'By the way, something you said rang a bell with me,' I said.

'Oh, yes. What?'

'You said that the Chuckle Brothers would slit your throat…'

I could see recognition dawning in her eyes. The bell rang with her too.

'Tilly?' she murmured.

'Yes,' I said.

'So Gavin is off the hook?'

'It seems so, though I think we can keep it to ourselves for now.'

This gang warfare was hotting up to a point where I ought to be doing something about it. I would ring David in the morning.

Thirty Six

'Good morning, Hugh,'

'Good morning, Brenda. How did you know it was me?'

'We've had a new phone system installed. It gives me the caller's number. It's all David's doing. A big change from Mr Day's system'

'Rhodri, Jacson and Davies have been dragged into the twenty-first century at last, then?'

'Something like that. Did you want to speak to David?'

''Yes, please.'

'One moment,' then a brief pause, followed by David's voice wishing me a good morning and checking my health and temper.

'I'm fine, thanks,' I said.

'How is the search for information going?' he asked.

'Very well. I think I've found most of what you wanted. There's enough to put at least two people in jail. This gang war is getting out of hand and there's nothing up here that's worth killing or being killed for, and that's the way it's going at the moment. Do you want me to give this information to the police or send it to you for you to do it?'

'There's no harm in giving it to the police, I'll leave the timing to you. I'll need a copy, though, if you're printing it out.'

He asked about Louise and I related about her rough treatment at the hands of Curtis Jandrell. I also told him about Glen's crash and hospitalisation. He was surprised at the change in Glen. He had known him as a heartless drug dealer, rather than the astute and reasonable man that I had met.

'Leopards don't change their spots, Mr Evans. Just watch your back.' was his final warning before we hung up.

My phone buzzed. It was Louise.

'Hugh, can you come and pick me up.' There was panic in her voice.

'Sure. On my way. What's up?' I asked, struggling to put on my coat and hold the phone to my ear at the same time.'

'Jimmy's dead,' What she said next was masked by a flood of emotion as tears started to flow. Tears at the loss of a friend? Tears of fear? Would she be next on Gavin's list? That thought had been with her for a couple of days. She needed protection.

'I'll be there soon,' I said. ' Don't let anyone in except me. Bye.'

I raced to my car and drove round to hers. The rush hour being over, the streets were relatively empty. I was among professional drivers, driving sensibly, rather than the commuters who drive just twice a day, confined to spells of sitting in impatient queues of traffic interspersed with brief periods of a mad rush, ducking and diving in and out of the traffic to avoid being late for work in the morning or getting home in the evening. I did a bit of ducking and diving myself, weaving through the steady stream, passing lorries and vans in my haste to get to Louise.

My mind was full of questions as I drove, not all of them with a satisfactory answer. What had happened to Jimmy? Natural causes? Doubtful. He seemed fit and well to me when last I saw him. Road accident? Impossible. He didn't drive, though pedestrians do sometimes get run over. Murdered? Unlikely unless the random killings of late could be escalating. Gavin had staged yesterday's fracas; was he cranking up the tension by acting out of turn. Not tit-for-tat any more. Or was Jimmy's killer nearer home? Very possible, in view of what Curtis might have perceived as insubordination at the meeting. That final reference to - 'some of you' - took on an ominous feel. Anything could have happened.

Louise rushed out of the house, locked the door and flew down the path to my car as I pulled up.

'Drive,' she commanded, as she fastened her seat belt and gave me directions as we went. Ten minutes later we arrived at a new tower block with a couple of police cars parked outside. An ambulance was just driving away.

I stayed in the car. Louise approached a constable.

'What happened to Jimmy?' she asked.

'He was found dead on the ground here at six o'clock this morning. That's all I know, miss. Did you know him?'

'We worked at the same place, the Dragon's Lair.'

'Oh, the casino.' he confirmed, and she nodded assent. He looked up the side of the tower, Louise followed his gaze up to the peaked cap of a policeman who was looking over the fifth-floor balcony. Still in the car, I craned to look up as well.

'You'd better wait here, miss. The Inspector might want a word with you. She'll be down in a minute.'

Louise got into the car to wait. A chilly wind was tugging at her hair and it was warmer inside, only slightly though, as the short journey had given the car heater no time to warm up. She needed to talk.

'Surely, he didn't jump from there. He didn't seem unhinged after the meeting. Just went home quietly. Yes, he was subdued. We all felt that way after Curtis's outburst. So if he didn't jump...' She left the sentence suspended, unfinished, leaving it to me to guess the alternative.

A couple of policemen and a lady came out of the front door of the block. Louise stepped out of the car to meet them. I slowly wound down the window,

'Have you any idea what happened?' Louise asked.

The constable from earlier moved across and explained to the inspector that she was a 'work colleague of the deceased'. A delicate way of putting it.

'Good morning, Mrs Sturgess. We meet again.'

Non-plussed for a moment, Louise gathered her wits and made the connection.

'Oh. It's DI Thorpe, isn't it? Sorry, I didn't recognise you.'

'I see your bruising has cleared up. So you worked with Mr Quayle?' Social chit chat over in a sentence, she quickly went back to work.

'We worked at the same place, yes,' Louise replied. 'I'm the Floor Manager in the casino, Jimmy worked in the office. Our paths crossed only occasionally.'

'In reply to your question, no, we don't know what happened at the moment. He didn't leave a note, so I think we can rule out suicide. Did he have any mental health issues? Depression, for instance?'

'Not that I'm aware of. We had a stormy meeting at work yesterday, but nothing to have brought on this result, I am sure.'

'The absence of a note is further evidence that it was not suicide,' the inspector said.

'Further evidence? Was there something else?'

' Yes. We're fairly sure he was murdered.'

Louise's expression asked for amplification.

'His door had been forced, splintered, in fact, and there was a rag stuffed into his mouth, no doubt to stop him shouting on the way down and alerting possible witnesses, giving the perpetrator a chance to escape unobserved.'

Louise and I both shuddered at the thought of Jimmy's brief discomfort as the rag was shoved into his mouth, wondering what was about to happen. I think we both hoped that it had been quick, that his torment had been short-lived, that he had not been tortured in any way before being flung over the edge of his balcony to certain death on the forecourt below.

The inspector moved over to my car.

'Another dead body. Another visit by Mr Evans,' she said. 'I would be ignoring all my training if I overlooked a possible connection. Would you like to explain your presence here?'

'Very simple,' I said. 'You will have noticed the increasing number of crimes committed recently, which seem to be connected to the two casinos. I have been visiting Mrs Sturgess, who works at one of them and has worked at the other. Her friend Tilly was murdered, hence your previous visit to check Gavin Scott's alibi, and now another of her work colleagues is murdered. She came to find out what had happened, to keep her employer informed. She was shaken by the news so she asked me to drive her over here. All her other friends are at work; I am on a break, I can hardly call it a holiday, and my time is my own. So here I am, chauffeur for the day, waiting to take her home. She's due in work at one o'clock, so she will need to freshen up and get into uniform.'

She seemed satisfied with my reply, even smiled at the 'chauffeur' reference. Louise got into the car and we drove off to her house.

I will need a little time to sort out the findings of my holiday before handing over to DI Thorpe. Sometime in the next couple of days would be soon enough. I had told no lies about my presence here. I just hadn't volunteered any extra information. Most importantly, I had raised no suspicions as to the real reason for my 'holiday'. Greater Manchester Police had drawn a blank over the overturned lorry. Denny Shaw could give them no lead as to the hirer of the lorry and Dan Brennan wasn't around to explain. Their investigation had stalled. I would be able to fill in the gaps in their information, but not yet. The police were not the only ones involved in the results of my enquiries, results which would have dire consequences for Curtis Jandrell and others.

187

I took Louise to the Dragon's Lair via her home to get ready for work. On the way, our discussion turned towards Jimmy's death. We both had our suspicions about the Chuckle Brothers; it had their stamp all over it. Having delivered Louise to work I drove to a nearby coffee shop.

As I waited to be served, a voice behind me said, 'This must be a popular place; you're here again.'

I turned around to identify the familiar voice – it was Ben Kealy's, on his own.

'Hello,' I said. 'Nice to see you again. No Charlotte today?'

'No, not today,' he replied.

'No Tinker either,' I observed. There was no dog tucked into his jacket today.

' No. Sadly, we lost him.'

'Oh, dear, what happened?'

'He became very ill and died last night. That's why Charlotte is at home. She's absolutely distraught. The vet diagnosed Parvo virus.'

I expressed my sympathy.

'Have you been in touch with the people you bought him from?' I asked.

'Yes, I rang this morning. Strange, really. When they answered, I told them who I was and that a pup I had bought had died. They put the phone down straight away. No comment. No sympathy. No money back offer. Nothing. Then I tried ringing again, thinking we'd been cut off or poor signal or something. But I couldn't get through. My number was blocked. I tried on Charlotte's phone but they must have recognised my voice as that went dead and was blocked later. Perhaps Charlotte should have spoken to them instead, but she was too overcome to speak to anyone. We don't know what to do next.'

I was in a quandary. I couldn't reveal what I knew about the operation. Ben was angry enough to do something about it, something which would warn them off enough to remove all trace of their existence at Hawthorn House.

On the other hand, my sympathies lay with those poor dogs, suffering in this way, the disease spreading not only within Sperrymoor Farm, but also out in the wider world to every dog they met on their daily walks.

The disappointment of the proud new owners was probably unbearable. I recalled how I felt when Nell was killed so many years ago. It never leaves you.

At least, Ben knew nothing of my mission here in Manchester, so had no expectation that I could do anything about his problem. I sympathised with him and shared a table as we drank our coffee. We agreed something ought to be done, but what? We left the problem undecided, the fate of so many problems where criminals were involved, where decent people can see no route to justice and so the crimes go on.

Ben and I shook hands on the car park.

'Tell you what,' I said. 'Let me have your number. Crazier things have happened, but if I come up with something I'll let you know. I'll ask our vet if he knows what you can do.'

Clutching at that tenuous straw, Ben told me his number.

Back in the car, I set the sat-nav to the postcode for Hawthorn House and drove off. Again racing through traffic, I was a man on a mission. I hoped that Ben would not be doing the same. His concern for Charlotte might keep him at home rather than tearing up to Hawthorn House to wreak retribution for their shattered dreams.

On familiar territory at last, I recognised the houses lining the road near to the shop where I had bought the Manchester Evening News. I rounded the bend where I had accosted Crystal's father and Rusty, next on the right was Hawthorn House. Feverish activity was going on, loading a small furniture van with the contents of the house. I drove on without staring, on to the busy yard of Cross's Cranes.

I parked and climbed the steps up to the first-floor office above the storeroom. The same young lady greeted me.

'Hello again. Have you come about the boat?'

Before I could answer, her phone rang.

'Cross's Cranes. Irene speaking. How can I help?' I heard a voice babbling at the other end. 'Yes, we do crane hire ,' she explained before becoming involved in a rambling discussion about crane hire, weight of the crane, what it could lift, how soon they can come and so on and on. She mouthed an apology to me; I signalled back to indicate that it was no problem; it suited me to have more time to observe the activity at Hawthorn House. Ben's call had rung alarm bells. The furniture was hurriedly loaded into the van by two men who I recognised as bouncers at the Dragon's Lair.

Bella rushed here and there with cardboard boxes, presumably crockery, linen, ornaments and other small items which had fooled so many customers into thinking it was a normal residence.

Irene finished her call. 'Sorry about that,' she said.

'No problem,' I replied. 'It looks like your neighbours are leaving,' I said, indicating Hawthorn House.

'Yes. I never see them, so they won't be missed. Now, your boat, how have you got on?

'Well, I'm sorry but I won't need your services after all. I told you I'm new to boating.' She nodded agreement.

I continued, 'I've found that there's a dry dock at a boatyard further down the canal. I can use that, so there's no need for a lift.

'That's OK, Thanks for letting me know.' Irene said. 'We'll be here if you need us in the future.'

'Thanks, then. I'd better be off.' We said our goodbyes and I left. The furniture van was pulling out of Hawthorn House when I was on the lane. I decided to follow it. I would have to keep my distance to avoid detection. As the scenery changed, I worked out that we were going up to the moors. I hung back, increasing the space between us. Sperrymoor Farm was obviously the destination. As I reached the vantage point from my first visit, I pulled off the road. Across the valley, I could see the furniture van climbing up to the farm and turning into the gateway. I had seen enough. I turned around and made my way back into Manchester.

Thirty Seven

This was turning out to be a busy day.

On the journey back, my phone rang. I answered it, hands free. It was Maldwyn Humphreys.

'Good news, Mr Evans. I hope it's not going to be too much of a rush.'

'A rush? Why?'

'The Home Office have arranged space on a cargo flight which leaves tomorrow from Manchester Airport. They only fly to Incheon once a week and tomorrow's the day. Take off is at 11.30am. There's no problem taking the coffins to Manchester, but can you get in touch with your friend to get her up here in time?'

'I'll do my best,' I said. 'Leave it with me. I'll ring you later.

There was not a minute to lose. I rang Grace and gave her the news. She was pleased, but needed to ring Park Jong-yop to let him know. Hopefully. the millionaire would find a slot at short notice in his busy schedule to travel up here to see his compatriots off on their last journey. She would ring me back. It had been a short call. As usual, I could hear her boss's voice, presumably complaining about staff taking personal calls at work.

My next port of call was the shopping mall. I was interested in finding out more about Just Computers. Had they moved in? Had they survived the affray? Who runs it now? Were there any more consignments from Ireland? I was becoming more inquisitive as time wore on.

I drove through the familiar, dismal streets which surrounded the original Just Computers shop. Was it less than a fortnight ago that I first discovered this area? The broken doors and empty windows, some charred by fire, were a signature of the street. Tenants had been forced out by the threat of fire or vandalism as the decreasing population lost its security in the absence of neighbours. In previous times, neighbours looked after each other. You could leave your door open while you popped to the shop; everyone knew each other's business, looked out for each other's kids; it had been a community.

I passed the remains of Darren's shop. The shattered window had not been boarded up; the door swung idly in the breeze, festooned in discarded police tape, the only colour in the otherwise monochrome street, ringing the ancient bell in a death knell for the whole street, it seemed.

But not the whole street. Farther along I saw a tall, black man entering a house and immediately, an old lady was pushed through the door on to the street. She turned to remonstrate with him but he pushed her further away, shouting and swearing as he did so, not listening to her protests. She staggered and fell, but he made no effort to help her up; he ignored her and re-entered the house. I drew up alongside her, leapt out of the car and helped her to her feet. Tears of frustration ran down her cheeks.

'I told him I'd be gone next week!' she cried.

'Told who?' I said.

'Mr Jandrell. My landlord. He said I could stay. My daughter is coming to help me. Why are these men here, throwing me out?'

'Men? There's more than one?'

'Yes. Two. Twins, I think. They both look the same.'

'Wait here,' I said. 'You can sit in my car, if you like.'

She nodded and shuffled towards the car.

'What's your name?' I enquired.

'Doreen. Doreen Eastley,' she replied as she settled into the passenger seat.

I walked into the house. There was a long hall-way with rooms off on either side. I turned right into a neat but sparse lounge where a tall man was holding a handbag, taking money from the purse. The few banknotes it contained could have been the remains of this week's pension that Mrs Eastley could ill afford to lose.

'Put that back,' I ordered.

Suddenly, my arms were pinned to my sides as another man emerged silently from the room across the hall and flung his arms around me, rendering me powerless, or so he thought. I dropped my head forward, then snapped it back violently. The cry of pain he let out told me that I had been accurate; the flow of warm blood down the back of my neck told me how accurate. I was sure it was his blood and not mine. The pain from his broken nose caused him to release his hold. I sprang free, spun around and took him by the throat in my left hand.

A thump in the ribs folded him over the back of the settee and I held my right fist threateningly above his face. I ordered the other man again, 'Put that back!' He hesitated, then looked at his brother's bloodied face, which was gasping for air like a landed fish, with the threat of my right fist about to rearrange his features. He decided that discretion was the better part of valour and returned the notes to the purse.

'What are you doing here?' I demanded.

'What's it got to do with you?' he shouted.

'Plenty.' I said, squeezing hard on his brother's windpipe, bringing a strangled scream from the prostrate one.

'The old lady has to go. Let's just say we're giving her a helping hand.' he said.

'Shoving her out on to the road is not helping her. Curtis said she could stay till next week.'

194

The use of his boss's Christian name suggested that I knew him well and might have some influence with him. I decided to cultivate that thought. I released my victim and took out my phone to ring Louise.

'Hi. I'm at Denman Street with Mrs Eastley.'

'Ye…es,' she replied, wondering where this was going.

'The Chuckle Brothers are here making a forced eviction. She says that Curtis had agreed for her to stay till next week and she's got it all arranged with her daughter. Can you get Curtis to call off the dogs for me, please?'

'Of course. Mrs Eastley at Denman Street you said?

'Yes.'

'I'll do it now,' she finished and the call was over.

I spent an uneasy five minutes, waiting with the Chuckle Brothers. Conversation was sparse.

'Which one of you is Obi, then?' I asked.

The handbag one, who now added surprise to the expressions on his face, said 'I am.'

'So you must be Dola,' I said to the one still tending his bleeding nose. He nodded, as surprised as his brother had been that I knew their names. They were unsure of my status. Perhaps I worked for Curtis as well, but higher up the organisation than they were.

Obi's phone buzzed. It was Curtis.

His message was short and sweet.

'Get out of there. Leave the lady alone.'

'But you said…'

'Don't argue. Get out of there.'

His voice had carried to all three of us. A man used to giving orders - and having them obeyed immediately, I guessed. A man who answered any question of his authority with violence. If I wanted evidence of it, I only had to recall Louise's bruised face and Jimmy's death, the results of talking back to his boss and accusing him of unfairness.

The Chuckle Brothers left in a hurry, not even acknowledging Mrs Eastley sitting in my car. Their car, a grey Mercedes, was parked further up the street and roared away as though it had been their idea to leave. They were probably glad to get away from a sticky situation, at the same time not looking forward to their next meeting with Curtis.

I went to my car.

'Come on, Doreen,' I said, 'They've gone and they won't be back. Mr Jandrell has called them off, so you're OK for next week.'

Tears of gratitude and relief filled her eyes.

'Thank you so much. I'm so grateful. Would you like a cup of tea?' Her eyes started to twinkle 'Or something stronger. I've got a little bottle of whisky in the cupboard.'

'No, thanks. I've got to be off. Glad to be of help. Good bye and good luck with the move next week.

As she shuffled into her neat little house, I drove off. I needed to shower and change my blood-stained shirt before my next call.

In the course of dressing again after the shower at my B&B, my phone rang. It was Grace.

'That was quick,' I observed.

'Yes. As I said before, Park Jong-yop is a multi-millionaire and he has put his PA on to it right away. I had explained all about it and where you fitted into things, so he suggested that he will come up in his private plane. He will pick me up at Sleap, a little airfield north of Shrewsbury and then we will fly to Barton Airfield, which is twenty minutes' drive from Manchester Airport.'

'That's brilliant,' I said. 'I can take you on from there,' but Grace continued.

'No need. If you and Mr Humphreys can meet us at Barton Airfield, we can all travel together. Park's PA, her name is Caroline, will organise a chauffeur-driven car for us.'

'Good. I will let Maldwyn Humphreys know this and he will need to ask the Home Office to arrange passes for us. Also, we will be airside, so we'll need an escort from the Airport staff. I'll let you know the times as soon as I can so that Park can sort out his flight plan. By the way, we will not be able to see the plane taking off. The public viewing area is about twenty minutes away from the freight terminal, but the plane will taxi to the runway in about ten minutes. We can bid farewell to Min-jun and his friends as it taxis away. We will not be allowed into the control tower, which would be the best vantage point, not with a group of four. I hope that will be all right.'

With assurances that it would, and with promises to keep in touch, the call ceased with a click.

I spoke then to Maldwyn, who was in agreement with the arrangements so far. He would get the Home Office moving immediately and was looking forward to receiving the times of the cargo flight and the arrival time of Park and Grace at Barton.

I felt that I could do with a PA to keep track of all these arrangements and phone calls as I continued with my original plan to visit Just Computers at the new Mall. There was plenty of free parking and I strolled into the Mall through the big swing doors which had miraculously survived the fighting. There were chairs and tables outside the Cosy Café again, to replace those damaged the day before. The next-door window had been repaired overnight; there was no trace of broken glass, indeed, there was no indication whatsoever of the mayhem that had taken place at the opening ceremony.

Further into the Mall I found a smartened-up Just Computers shop. This time it carried a wide range of accessories with glowing offers on ink cartridges, printers and office supplies. Having gazed into the window for a short time, I went into the shop to be met by a bright young man, mid-twenties, I guessed, eager to sell me something.

'What is it you're looking for?' he asked. 'I saw you spending some time at the window.'

'I was wondering whether you had received another consignment of computers yet. Darren said he was expecting some in after his others were lost in transit.'

'Oh, Darren Jandrell? He got killed, didn't he? I never knew him. Yes, another load arrived ready for the opening ceremony. Can I show you one?'

'Did you say Jandrell? Was he related to …?'

He jumped in.

'Curtis Jandrell? He was his son.'

He kept that quiet, I thought. When we chatted, he had only referred to 'the owner' with no indication that it was his father. Curtis obviously wanted the connection kept secret.

A change of tack was necessary.

'Do you maintain the casino computers, like Darren did?'

'Yes. It's a massive undertaking.'

I looked up at a row of certificates on the wall. He was obviously proud of his achievements. An Honours Degree from Manchester University stood next to a Diploma in Software Engineering followed by membership of the British Computer Society. An impressive array.

His name also rang bells. On each certificate in italic handwritten script was inscribed Brian Archibald Moffatt.

I didn't have to ask how he got the job. Keeping it in the family seemed to be the way they work round here.

198

Thirty Eight

Feverish telephone activity between Maldwyn, Grace and Park's PA, Caroline with me in the middle had resulted in a workable schedule for today's appointment at Manchester Airport.

Park Jong-yop would fly up from a private airfield in Surrey to arrive at Sleap in Shropshire, just north of Shrewsbury, to pick up Grace at 12 noon. He will then fly on to Barton Airfield via the Low Level Corridor, avoiding the traffic for the international airports at Manchester and Liverpool, to arrive before 13.30. Maldwyn and I will arrive separately at Barton for 13.30 as well and the chauffeur-driven car will take us all to the freight area at Manchester Airport. We would be in time to see the coffins and urns loaded on to the Korean Air aircraft before it taxied away to take off at 14.30. Fourteen hours later, they would be home.

Maldwyn and I waited at Barton, watching the sky for the arrival of Park's Piper Archer. We needn't have worried; he arrived in good time. Caroline had done an excellent job of informing everyone concerned as to what was happening, though I suspect that the TV cameraman alighting from his van had found out what we were doing from his company's devious means, not from Caroline. We had no desire for publicity. She had notified airfield managements in good time so that Park could leave his pride and joy in a secure parking space, ready for his departure. The uniformed chauffeur met us at the gate, waiting patiently while introductions took place.

Park was a smartly dressed man in his mid-thirties. He smiled a welcome as Grace introduced us. He shook hands warmly, all round, thanking us all for our kindness to his unfortunate countrymen and women.

In turn, I thanked him for his generosity both in paying for the repatriation and for bringing Grace from Shrewsbury. She assured me that she was quite excited to travel in a private plane, especially at an altitude from which she could see the landscape with familiar landmarks of towns and lakes.

We moved over to the freight terminal with the TV cameraman tagging along behind. We were escorted on to airside by a yellow-coated airport employee named Megan, who firmly denied access to the TV man, who had turned up too late to arrange an airside pass. Megan had been briefed as to the purpose of our visit and told us that she felt a little embarrassed to be wearing a yellow high-vis jacket on what was effectively a funeral occasion, so separated herself from our group. I knew how she felt. I had managed to buy a black tie to mark the occasion from a charity shop near the B&B, but, otherwise, I had only casual clothes with me. However, Park had brought his camera and prevailed upon Megan to take photos of our group so that he could relay it to the authorities in Korea, with descriptions of what we had done to assist in the return of the remains of their loved ones. She would make sure not to include any commercially sensitive details.

We stood in a line, amazed as at least a dozen aircraft of the world's airlines were being loaded from the long warehouse behind us. The coffins were brought out by a fork lift, on pallets, three at a time and delivered to the hold of the blue-topped Korean Air Cargo plane with its Pepsi-like logo on the tail. As a smaller coffin passed us. Grace looked at me.

'Eun-jung,' she whispered as tears rolled down her cheeks.

I nodded agreement, thinking of the child crawling over the bodies of people who had been her friends for a final cuddle with her brother, seeking safety and comfort in his arms.

Finally, all was safely aboard, the doors were locked, the plane was pushed back and the long journey home began. Park saluted as the aircraft moved towards the taxiway; I raised a hand in farewell (an incongruous term in the circumstances), as did Maldwyn; Grace's tear-stained handkerchief fluttered in the breeze as she raised it.

'Annyeonghi gaseyo' she said.

I needed no translation of 'Goodbye'.

Then they were gone.

Thirty Nine

That evening, at the B&B, I rang Bethan. She sounded very much like her old self when she answered.

'How are you and Jess getting on?' I asked.

Life was wonderful, she told me, though she wished that I had been there to share in the enjoyment. She had made some good friends, fellow walkers. Even their dogs got on well together.

'I just wish I could stop worrying about you, though,' she said.

'I'm fine,' I said, and went on to tell her about some of the things that had happened, well abridged, sanitised, you might say. Apart from the scuffle with Dola Chukwu, there had been nothing hand-to-hand to report, bullets and bombs had passed me by, so I could make light of my involvement in the life of Manchester in the last two weeks.

'I'm sure you're not telling me everything,' she said and I could picture the wry smile which crossed her pretty face. 'You can save the gory details until we get home.' I have said before, she knows me so well.

Changing the subject, I said that the Koreans had been repatriated.

'That was quick. I thought they had to find a lot of money. That would take time, surely?'

'It would have done,' I replied, 'but a Korean millionaire from Surrey paid it all for them. He even brought Grace up to

Manchester in his private plane to see them off. Maldwyn Humphreys and I were there as well. It was all very sad and touching.'

'Grace would have enjoyed the flight, I'm sure, even though it was a sad occasion,' she said.

I went on to tell her that I would need more time up here. A couple of meetings would see my job finished so that I would be able to return home at the weekend. This produced the usual dichotomy. She didn't want the holiday to end, but she would also be glad to get home once more. Fortunately, she appreciated the extra time and there would be no problem with her accommodation.

Our call came to an end as we made arrangements for meeting at Shrewsbury Station at the end of the week.

I found Natalie Thorpe's card and rang her number, though I didn't expect to find her at the office. I was preparing to leave a message.

'Hello. DI Thorpe.' she was entitled to sound tired. It was nine o'clock, after all.

'Hi, it's Hugh Evans. I wonder if you can find some time to see me tomorrow morning. It's important or I wouldn't be ringing at this time of the evening.'

She consulted her diary and after some thought, she said, 'How about eight o'clock, or is that too early for you?'

Eight o'clock was fine with me.

'Any reason why? We don't get people asking to come in to a police station. We usually have to drag them in!'

'I'd like to bring you up to date with what I've been doing. You may find it helpful.'

'Intriguing,' she said. 'I look forward to it. To be honest, I was going to ask you to come in tomorrow, anyway.'

I returned her question.

'Any reason why?'

'I was watching the Northern News on TV tonight and there was coverage of the Korean immigrants' bodies being returned home. And there, in the middle of it, was none other than Hugh Evans. As I said, intriguing. We'll talk more in the morning.'

Forty

Next morning, Detective Inspector Natalie Thorpe got up from behind her desk and shook my hand in welcome. A nice informal start to our meeting. I sat facing her across the empty desk.

'Let me begin by telling you what I know,' she said. I listened with interest.

'I first heard of you from DI Humphreys when he gave me the number of a lorry which had been involved in people smuggling and had crashed on his patch. He said that you had found it and reported it to him. He spoke well of you, so I felt I could trust you. I traced the vehicle to Denny Shaw's but as it was a hired lorry, Denny knew nothing about its use and had no information about its hirer.'

'Yes, Maldwyn told me your investigation had stalled.' I said.

'Then you turned up at Just Computers, sole witness to a shooting. We met again at Mrs Sturgess's home Then you showed up on CCTV of the car bomb at the Dragon's Lair and again after the fatality at the flats. As I mentioned last evening, I saw you on TV, at the departure of the Korean victims of the lorry crash. What I am having difficulty with is how these events are connected, where you seem to be a step ahead of us each time. So, I am hoping you can make some sense of it for me.'

'I'll do my best,' I said, I began with my personal background in the Army and then at Llanynder school. This led on to how I had become involved with the lorry, via the bottle the children had brought me.

'At about the same time, a young man, an ex-pupil of the school from many years ago, turned up. He had been a solicitor in Manchester but had returned to his roots in Wales. His name is David Pearce.'

She thought for a moment.

'I think I may have come across him in court,' she said.

'Possibly. His wife was shot in a drive-by shooting some years ago, and he asked me if I could come to Manchester to make some enquiries on his behalf. He didn't really say why. He told me to contact an old friend as she might be a useful source of information because she worked in a casino.'

'Ah, Mrs Sturgess.' The penny was beginning to drop.

'The lorry had contained a consignment of computers as a cover for the trip, to be delivered to Just Computers. That was my first port of call. The shooting happened while I was there. There was some rivalry between the two casinos, the Golden Rainbow and the Dragon's Lair, partly because I heard that Glen Dalby thought that Curtis Jandrell had shopped him over the drugs deal that put him in jail. When he came out this gang war took off. Darren was killed, followed by Tilly, that's Matilda Bolton, you'll remember, then the bomb and Glen's crash. Then there was the ruckus at the opening of the Mall.'

'This is useful information, giving us the whys and wherefores over the killings,' Natalie interjected, then I went on.

'David wanted to know where Curtis Jandrell had got his money from. My chat with Darren gave me some leads, plus Mrs Sturgess had a useful input, and I found that apart from the casino, he owned Just Computers and a farm, as well as a lorry firm, possibly Denny's, and the people smuggling.'

'A farm? We didn't know about that.' She was surprised.

'Yes, Sperrymoor Farm on the moors. Not agricultural, though. I've been up there. It's a puppy farm. Terrible conditions. They were selling the pups via the classifieds in the papers possibly to pet shops as well. I've seen the house where they sell the pups, but they've recently moved out to avoid detection. They also have Parvo virus. I've spoken with one of their customers who lost a puppy recently. Will it be you or the Council who need to take action?'

'It sounds as though we'd better get up there to investigate as soon as we can. The Council will want to prosecute for unlicensed selling afterwards. We'll have to get the RSPCA in on it as well. Immediately.'

She picked up her phone, 'Have you got a minute, Dave?' and put the phone down. A fresh-faced young detective, DS Dave Kirk, looking too young to be a sergeant, came in.

'Yes, boss' he said.

'Get two teams together. Two cars. We're going up the moors.'

'Yes, boss,' he said again and left, enthusiastically. Up the moors was better than looking at a screen all day.

Natalie tapped a few keys on her keyboard to find a contact at the RSPCA, then dialled the number.

'Roger? Natalie Thorpe. I've just heard of an illegal puppy farm. We're going up there now. Can you and your vet make your way up there as well? It's Sperrymoor Farm.'

I scribbled the postcode on a piece of paper and pushed it across the desk to her and she repeated it to Roger. She put the phone down.

'You can come too,' she said as she donned her coat. 'You can tell me the rest of your exploits on the way.'

The drive up to Sperrymoor Farm could be classed as thrilling. It reminded me of Army days, with highly trained drivers manoeuvring through the morning traffic as though it wasn't there. I told Natalie that there was probably no need to rush as the place was deserted most of the time. She replied with a 'You never know' kind of answer and pressed on. On the way, she radioed the other car and briefed them as to the purpose of our journey. Of course, she was right.

Our convoy wound its way on to the moors, following Roger of the RSPCA with three volunteers in the leading car, followed by the two police cars.

As we made our way down to the hairpin at the bottom of the valley, in full view of the farm, our approach had been noted and frantic activity was going on at the farm. The gate was flung open and the white van sped out and turned to go up on to the moor. Roger turned into the gate and the leading police car was quickly on the heels of the van. In splitting his attention between staying on the tarmac and peering into his mirrors, the van driver veered off the narrow road and into a boggy patch which stopped him dead. A quick arrest was made and he was brought back to the farm in the police car.

Our car turned into the yard and yellow high-vis police jackets appeared all over the property. Roger stood in the doorway of the cage room, which had been left unlocked in their haste, not allowing anyone in while one of his volunteers did something, I'm not sure what, up near the house. Eventually, he gave the all-clear for his volunteers, clad in blue, hooded, disposable head to foot coveralls, to go in.

'You can't be too careful with Parvo virus about,' he explained to Natalie, as she stood in the doorway of the cage room, taking in the scene. All the dogs barked in their excitement at the horde of visitors which had arrived. The noise was deafening. The white van driver was hand-cuffed and taken into the house to be held in the sparsely furnished lounge with two other men who he had left stranded when he left. They were just a little pleased to see him, he who had left them in the lurch. Two constables watched over them, one by the French window, one at the door, while DS Dave Kirk arranged for a van to be brought up to take them to the station and meanwhile took down their particulars.

Roger's vet, Jim Watson arrived and inspected the scene inside the cage room, where Roger's blue-clad volunteers were hard at work cleaning dogs and pens. It was a massive task.

'How on earth can people do this to dogs?' Jim asked, not expecting an answer, as he took in the carnage before him. Dogs with a thick coat were matted with faeces. Water bowls were empty. Floors had not been swept for days and probably not washed for months. Urine-soaked newspapers lay in the cages, pellets of dog food strewn amongst the papers and faeces. The smell of ammonia was overpowering. Dead puppies, of various breeds, lay on a box at the one end, victims of the virus.

'They haven't even got the decency to bury them, Jim' Roger remarked to his vet, who was shaking his head ruefully. Jim found it difficult to believe what he was looking at, even though he had seen scenes like this before.

I asked Roger about Parvo virus.

'It's a killer,' he said. 'It's found in pups from six to twenty weeks of age. If they can weather it for three or four days, they can make a complete recovery, but as the owners are often inexperienced with dogs, the treatment is sought too late to do any good.'

'So how do they catch it?' I asked.

'Contact with other infected dogs, so places like this are high on the list. So are dog shows, playing in the park, anywhere they can meet another dog. Even on faeces, shoes, clothes, bedding, shared bowls, carpets, etcetera, etcetera. The virus can survive up to six months in such surroundings, so a replacement pup is at risk if introduced too soon into the home. Doting parents who say 'I'll get you another one, dear' are not doing the pups any favours and are leaving their child open to another crushing disappointment.'

Jim returned from inside, his frustration showing on his face. 'This keeps happening, Roger,' he said, 'and as soon as you close one down another springs up despite the heavy sentences and relieving them of their ill-gotten gains under proceeds of crime rules. There's a thriving import-export trade as well. Add in the theft of dogs in this country and you're looking at a multi-million-pound industry.'

Natalie walked out on to the yard, her handkerchief to her eyes, whether this was due to ammonia or emotion I was not sure.

'I'll leave this area to you, Roger. I think I'll go back to the station and speak to these men. You can come too,' she said to me. 'You can tell me how this works. Surely nobody comes here to buy a pup? They'd never buy one after seeing those conditions.'

'Very true,' I said. 'No, they have a house, isolated from its neighbours, to which the customers come to see the pups. Whether that's owned or rented I don't know. They furnish just one room, usually the kitchen, so it's bright and impressive. Plus the downstairs toilet.'

'Why the toilet?'

'If the customers have travelled a long way, or they have children with them, they might ask to use the toilet - kids always do. It's all the pent-up excitement of getting a puppy I think - so it's kept clean and tidy so as not to arouse suspicion. The lady of the house does all the selling. Again, a smart, presentable lady, giving the impression of a respectable home. Viewings are all by appointment, so that they bring the right pup down from the farm.

'How do they know which pup to bring?' Natalie asked.

'Each advert is for a specific breed, with a separate phone number. When the customer rings, they know immediately which breed to talk about, confirming the impression that it's a private breeder with one dog. It's all about respectability.'

As if on cue, a constable came down the road from the stranded van, carrying a cardboard box.

'I think you ought to see these, ma'am. We'll bring the van down later,' he said, wondering what to do with the box.

'Here, I'll take it,' I said.

We looked into the box. Natalie put her latex gloves on and examined the contents.

'Mobile phones. A dozen of them.' she said.

'Turn one over,' I said. She did. On the back was written SPANIEL in white marker pen ink. The others bore other breed names.

'I see what you mean,' she said. 'We can finger-print these to nail down our suspects.'

'But they won't be the ones to benefit from the sales. We need the boss man. I suspect that will be Curtis Jandrell,' I put in.

'Why him?'

'He owns the farm. Some of the operatives are his employees. I think he gets the proceeds.' Open and shut, I thought.

'Except that he'll deny it. We'll have to have solid proof to make it stick.'

'Looking at his books might help, though they have been doctored by a real professional adviser, Archie Moffatt. I think HMRC may be interested in the books as well. Massive undisclosed income. Possible money laundering.'

Natalie was surprised. 'How do you know that?'

'Every Friday, his employee, the late Jimmy Quayle, went home to the Isle of Man for the weekend. He also took a bag of money with him and deposited it with Cayman Wealth Management.'

'You are remarkably well-informed, Mr Evans.'

'Just the result of my enquiries. I followed Jimmy to Douglas last week.'

'Was this the same Jimmy Quayle who fell from a height at the flats?'

'Yes.'

She rolled her eyes. 'There's a back-story there, then. You seem to have done all our work for us. We ought to sit down and get the rest of your story down on paper. For now, let's see what these men have to say.'

We left and returned to the station in readiness for their arrival. She took the opportunity to make a few calls. She was saying '…and get DS Moradi in to see me,' as we pulled into the police yard.

Forty One

We sat in Natalie's office once more, with mugs of hot coffee from the machine in the corner.

'I do appreciate your assistance here,' she began. 'Very often amateur investigators and sometimes professional private detectives get in our way, muddying the waters, making our jobs difficult. Fortunately, you seem to have done nothing detrimental to our work, in fact, you have made it easier in some ways. We did have our suspicions about you, you know.'

I was surprised to hear this and my face must have given that impression.

'It was a natural reaction to events. Questions at every step of the way.' She went on as if ticking off items on a list.

'You were the sole witness to the shooting, or did you do the shooting? Audacious enough to stay there and wait for us to turn up? It has been known. How often has the perpetrator, even in murder cases, helped the police at the start of the investigation? Then you gave Gavin Scott, a well-known shady character, an alibi. How strong was that? Guilt by association? You were clearly innocent of the car bomb. You wouldn't have done what you did to put the fire out if you had been the bomber. Or perhaps you would after the damage had been done. You turn up at Jimmy Quayle's flat and you were at the airfield. Again, innocent behaviour. But how come you did a trip to Southampton for Denny Shaw? That has me puzzled.'

I put my thoughts in order before I replied.

'When I arrived here, David Pearce had asked me to check up on Denny Shaw's company. We had found a delivery note of his in the lorry that overturned. The only way I could get to see Denny was to apply for a job - he had a sign up saying he was hiring drivers - so that was my way in and a couple of days later he asked me to do a special run for him. Nothing more suspicious than that.'

'But we were still unsure about you. You could have been carrying illegals as part of this network within the country moving them about.'

'Like Josh Redfern, you mean?'

She rolled her eyes again.

'Something else you need to tell me?'

'Later, perhaps. What convinced you that I wasn't?'

She picked up the phone. 'Ask DS Moradi to come in, please.'

The door opened and a bearded man came in. He turned to face me. It was Afran!

'Hello, Hugh,' he said.

I was lost for words. An undercover cop! Should I have been pleased to see him or annoyed about the subterfuge? On balance, I chose the first option. I had liked Afran on our short acquaintance.

'It's nice to see you. You're out of hospital. What about your injuries?' I asked.

'I was badly bruised and I had a dislocated shoulder. Some painful treatment and a night in hospital put me right. I'm back on duty.'

'But the story about your brother, was it true?'

'Yes, unfortunately, he is very ill. I had travelled there on duty and took the opportunity to visit him.'

'On duty. Your duty was to check on me. And what about your Khanjar? Was that true? I still have it in my car.'

'Yes. All true. I'm glad you looked after it for me.'

'Now I can return it.' I said.

214

'I'll see you when you finish here,' he said and went back into the outer office.

Natalie continued where she had left off.

'So you see, we had to check on you and found that you were a spectator, not a perpetrator. I'll want to see you again, Mr Evans,' Natalie said. 'There are still some loose ends. Will tomorrow morning be convenient?'

'Yes, of course,' I agreed.

I was unlikely to be allowed to observe the questioning of the men arrested at the farm, so I made my way out to the yard, where my car was waiting. On the way out through the office I signalled to Afran that I was leaving and he followed me out.

I opened my car door and retrieved the Khanjar from the door pocket. The sheath glinted in the sun as I handed it over.

'There you are,' I said, 'Safe and sound.'

'Thank you, my friend,' Afran said. 'I hope I can call you my friend. You looked after this for me, even though I gave you a fright with it on our journey. As we chatted through the journey, I could tell you were not involved in crimes and I didn't like hiding my real identity from you. But it had to be done.'

'I understand. Just doing your job,' I replied with a smile. 'I enjoyed your company, at least until the Khanjar came out.'

We laughed, shook hands and I got into the car.

Forty Two

My work here was almost done, though I had found out little about Curtis Jandrell. He was secretive in the extreme. His appearance at the Mall opening was a one-off. I would like to have found out more about him for David. I had told Natalie about the puppy operation, but nothing about Bella playing the part of the 'respectable lady' selling the puppies and delivering the money on Friday mornings. The Chuckle Brothers needed a mention too, Jimmy's death struck me as their style, Tilly's too. There would be another opportunity on the following day to bring her up to date.

I drove up to Sperrymoor Farm for the second time that day and found that Roger was very much in charge. He had mobilised some of his volunteers to come and clean up the cages and to groom some of the dogs.

'We'll have to leave them here for now; there are too many to transfer to kennels elsewhere but it will take some organising,' he explained, 'We can look after them here. New padlocks on the doors will keep others out. When we find out who the owner is, we can get him to sign them over to us and then we can take them away.'

I noticed yellow police jackets in the house.

'I don't think they'll find anything incriminating in there, it's only used for storage and making tea, as far as I know,' I said.

'Fingerprints will help to establish who's been here, especially if someone's denying their connection with this hell-hole.' Roger was obviously deeply affected by the conditions he found here.

'Some of my volunteers were in tears at the state the dogs were in. They wanted to move them right away, but we can't do that without the owner's permission. We only have your word that it's Curtis Jandrell. Have you any evidence for it? I can't go round accusing people without some proof.'

I had only Louise's word for the existence of a farm; Darren's invoice for installation of the CCTV, addressed to Curtis, showed that the casino owner also owned Sperrymoor Farm. I reached into my car and retrieved the red folder that was my filing system for times like this, and took out the copy invoice from Darren's shop.

'Will this be enough proof?' I asked, adding 'I haven't shown it to the police yet. I'm sure they'll be interested as well.'

'Too true. You hang on to it and give it to Natalie Thorpe when you see her tomorrow. Seeing it is good enough for me.'

'By the way,' I said, 'What about the CCTV? Won't they have seen this morning's activity if they're following it on the internet?'

'They might have seen their men making off but then it will have gone blank.'

'Why?' I asked.

'Because one of my volunteers was an electrician. He advised us to hold back until he found the right cable. We've met this kind of thing before. It didn't take him long to find the cable and cut it as it came out of the house. They'll be frantically wondering what has happened. They might well be expecting us, especially if they are unable to contact the men that Natalie arrested. They'll be very good at adding two and two. This time it will make four.'

I smiled grimly at his phraseology as we walked out away from the ammonia, which was slowly being overtaken by the equally overpowering smell of disinfectant. Across the valley, I could see a red Range Rover slowly executing a three-point-turn in the layby where I had parked on my first visit. We had been observed, and at that range a decent pair of binoculars would have enabled the owner to identify us individually and a report sent to Curtis. Great care would be needed from now on when Curtis received their report. He would surely respond in his usual violent way.

Forty Three

On the return journey from the moors, I phoned Louise.

'What are you doing for dinner this evening?' I enquired.

'Popping into town for a bit of late night shopping and grabbing a sandwich. I've had a busy day, so a bit of retail therapy is on the cards. I'd also like to pay a visit to the hospital to see Glen. I haven't been for a few days. He'll be getting bored with the inactivity.'

'Mind if I tag along? My treat for dinner, perhaps more than a sandwich. And I wouldn't mind visiting Glen.'

'Sounds good. Pick me up at 4:30 at the casino.'

And that was where Curtis spotted me on his CCTV, picking up Louise and driving away into town.

The shopping part of Louise's itinerary was reduced to a visit to a supermarket for a carton of milk, a pack of bacon and half a dozen eggs. That was breakfast sorted. Plus a bunch of grapes and a box of chocolates for Glen. The potentially longer visit to a ladies' dress shop was postponed until she would not have the encumbrance of a male trying not to look bored while she tried on yet another dress, then settling for the first one she had tried on.

We dined at a high street pizza parlour where we shared a spicy pizza with salad and coleslaw. After coffee, we set off for the hospital, where we found Glen remonstrating with Gavin. The discussion was getting heated as we walked in and Glen was doing his best to talk calmly to Gavin, who, in turn, was getting more irate.

'We can't let 'em get away with this,' Gavin was saying as he paced around the room. 'They'll be walking all over us.'

'No, we've got to take it quietly. Softly, softly, catchee monkey.' Glen replied. 'In the first place I'm stuck in here. Secondly, there's no point doing something big, like blowing up a car as that only alerts the police and thirdly, most importantly, I'm the boss and I say what we do.'

'I ran the firm when you were inside, didn't I?'

'You did. A lot of what you did was good, but you're too hasty sometimes. Hot-headed is the word. Just calm down.' Gavin was not placated.

Louise could see Glen getting paler.

'I think Glen's getting tired,' she said. 'Perhaps you could continue this another time.'

Glen nodded his agreement.

'It doesn't end here. We've got to do it my way.' Gavin retorted, 'It's the only way to keep them down.'

'Come on, Gavin,' Louise said, taking his elbow and steering him towards the door. 'You need to think about it further, on your own and Glen needs to rest in peace and quiet.' She led him out into the corridor, where he was reluctant to give up the argument.

Glen looked across at me. 'Gavin's got one on him this afternoon. Have you ever been in hospital? It's the very devil when you can't get out to do things.'

'Only once,' I said, holding up my right hand. 'It was for stitches only, so it wasn't a long stay. The operation was successfully achieved in a muddy gateway in the Falklands when a mine went off. They were cut off by a flying stone.'

'You were unlucky. Wrong place, wrong time.'

'Not as unlucky as my mate. It was Phil who stepped on the mine. He didn't come back.'

'Oh, sorry,' said Glen.

'It was a long time ago.'

We subsided into silence. The voices in the corridor were becoming louder as Gavin got angrier. I stepped through the door.

Gavin had Louise by the throat, pushing her against the wall. She was unable to speak. He was shouting, threatening.

'Stay out of things. You don't belong with us. If I see you near the Rainbow again, I'll ...'

'No you won't,' I said, stepping forward and flinging an arm around his neck from behind. 'Let her go!' I commanded.

'Or else what?'

'Or else I'll break your neck,' I said, tightening my grip, cutting off his air supply with a hint of promise of things to come as the pain in his vertebrae increased. He released his hold on her.

I had the tiger by the tail. I didn't let go.

'You're going to walk away, now, down that corridor and out. You can come back to see Glen when you've settled down. Understand?'

He knew when he was beaten. He nodded as best he could as my arm was still wrapped tightly around his neck.

Hospital corridors are notoriously long. It was the longest walk of Gavin's life as I watched him all the way down to Reception and out through the swing doors. He turned around a couple of times but as I was still watching, he continued walking. Knowing him as I do, I'm sure he would have been plotting all the way out.

Back in Glen's room, Louise enquired what the row was about.

'He's got a thing about explosives, lately. His mate did a break-in at a quarry in Derbyshire and has become flavour of the month with Gavin. He only wants to set a bomb off in the Dragon's Lair, preferably when Curtis is inside it. I've told him that popularity, like everything else, goes round in cycles. All you need is patience and don't panic. We'd lose all our customers if we got a reputation for killing everybody who upsets us, but he doesn't see it that way. And because the police had to let him go after Tilly was killed, he thinks he's fireproof. I confess, I made the mistake of saying, in one idle moment, that if Louise hadn't left, we'd still be popular.'

'So now he hates me more than ever,' Louise put in.

'I'm afraid so. But thanks for taking him outside. As I said to Hugh, it's frustrating to be stuck in here.'

He appreciated the grapes and chocolates. His ex-wife ignored him and his staff were unsure whether or not to visit, so Louise's gifts and company brought a pleasing ending to his day. And she had defused the row that had been building up when we arrived.

Our conversation visited all sorts of topics. Glen was surprised to hear that I am a school caretaker; he even offered me a job on security in his casino. I said that they hadn't printed enough money to tempt me away from my valley in Wales. We chatted on for nearly an hour, until visiting time ended and we had to leave.

Glen held Louise's hand in his free left hand. Sincerity was written all over his face. 'Thanks for coming. It's been great. Promise me, you'll be very careful. I don't trust Gavin. He might take it into his head to do something stupid. So be careful. Please.'

'I will. I promise. And Hugh will look out for me while he's here, I know,' she said, and kissed him on the cheek. I nodded my agreement, though I knew that my time in Manchester was close to the end.

I drove to Louise's home and checked outside and in for any hint of Gavin. Satisfied that she would be safe, I left.

Forty Four

Next morning, as I waited for the Full English part of Bed and Breakfast, I rang Louise to make sure she had had an uneventful night.

'Yes. I slept like a baby. I've got an early start today. I should be on my way now. Can we meet for lunch?' She was obviously in a rush.

'OK. Sounds good. You're in a hurry. We'll talk later.'

'Bye,' she said and was gone.

It was later in the morning that I received a text message from Louise.

Need you now. Whapshott Mill was all it said. It sounded like a problem, an urgent problem. My thoughts centred on Gavin. Has he kidnapped her? What evil plan has he come up with? Perhaps she should not have intervened last night. It's put her in danger. Where on earth is Whapshott Mill?

To answer the last question, I asked my landlady.

'It's a derelict building the other side of the Dragon's Lair casino' she said. 'Next to the canal. You can't miss it. I can't think why anybody would want to go there.'

I thanked her and made a hurried exit. I drove over to the casino, cursing the slow morning traffic as I went.

Whapshott Mill was not only derelict, there was no movement, it was deserted, as far as I could see. I cautiously walked into the cavernous body of the building and found pools of water on the grimy floor, each one adjacent to an empty canal-side window frame, where rain had blown in. Pipework, long redundant, was hung with thick, black cobwebs. The spiders had been busy, undisturbed for years. The silence was eerie; even the traffic noise from the road was inaudible. My footsteps echoed as I crossed the floor towards a door, which had probably been the office door in the hey-day of the mill's existence. I gently pushed it open. Something rustled. Rats?

There were no windows, I peered into the pitch blackness to no avail. Even when I stepped inside, I could still see nothing. I reached for my mobile to operate the torch to improve the situation. Too late! A heavy blow on the back of my head knocked me to the floor.

Later, I do not know how much later, I slowly recovered consciousness. There was still complete blackness. My hands were tied behind my back. My head was throbbing with the pain of the blow. I sensed something - or someone - lying on the floor beside me. Above the smell of dereliction, another aroma came through, a familiar aroma, Louise's aroma. Was she in here too? I moved my legs and touched something. I nudged with my knee and was rewarded with an answering grunt.

'Louise? Is that you?'

Another grunt. I took it as a 'yes'.

'Have you been gagged?' I asked.

Another affirmative grunt.

There was no point in asking further questions. And no need. The answers were about to arrive. The door opened and two men, silhouetted against the light, came in.

'Come with me, pretty lady,' one said. I recognised his voice. It was Obi Chukwa. 'You will be mine.' There was no mistaking his intentions. He untied Louise's hands and I could see in the limited illumination that came from the door, that he rolled her on to her back, then re-tied her hands together in front of her. Louise struggled but was no match for two men, one holding her hands, one holding her legs, preparing for what was to come. They were too strong for her and breathing through the gag was difficult. Grunts and stifled screams were all I heard.

'OK brother. You were born first. It is your privilege. I will be second. There will be time before Curtis comes.' Dola pulled her hands above her head and held them where they could do no harm to his brother. Louise struggled, kicked, grunted and screamed, to no avail.

I squirmed around until I could aim a kick at the head of the kneeling Dola. In the semi-darkness, accuracy was difficult and I missed, my foot only hitting his shoulder. He caught my raised foot with both hands, twisted it and pushed hard, so that I rolled painfully away into the dark corner of the room. Her hands now freed, Louise swung them over her head, and delivered a two-handed blow on the back of Obi's neck. It was hardly enough to stop him, despite catching him off-guard.

Suddenly, a voice rang out.

'Right, then. Are they here?'

A figure appeared in the doorway.

It was Curtis.

The brothers scrambled to their feet and hoisted us up and pushed us roughly out of the door. Blinking in the bright light, we were pushed across into another room which was furnished, to use the word loosely, with a table and three chairs - one on one side of the table and two facing it on the other - all four items thick with dust that was probably as old as the mill itself. Curtis took the single chair; we were forced into the others.

He signalled to the two men standing behind our chairs to leave. He was now in complete control of the situation. They left. I turned my head as they went.

'Bye, Obi. Bye, Dola.' I said. Even if the tiger has you in his jaws, it's always best to give him a tweak now and then.

225

The departing brothers turned and scowled, in response to my farewell. Curtis snarled 'Get out!' and they went.

'Nice couple of lads, aren't they? Helping an old lady to move house. Must have been Boy Scouts,' I said, conversationally. 'Are you going to tell us what's this all about or is it a guessing game?'

Curtis, wearing his hoodie, as always, must have felt that I was taking over chairmanship of this meeting, but he needed the upper hand. I went on.

'Are there any questions you would like to ask, because Louise will be unable to respond with a gag in her mouth. So how about you removing it?'

He clearly didn't like that, but common sense prevailed. As if to assert his authority, he was not gentle and Louise cried out as he roughly removed the gag. He resumed his seat on the other side of the table.

'Now are you going to tell us why we're here? I can't think of anything that Louise has done to deserve this and I have only helped out when your car was bombed. So, what have I done?'

His fingers drummed on the table as his temper grew. The prisoner was becoming interrogator. Curtis was used to being obeyed. His rule of iron, fists before talk, had kept him in control of his businesses all these years. He leaned across the table.

'I'll tell you what you've done.' He snarled. 'You've ruined my life. I have suffered a life of ridicule because of you. Even when I came up here to Manchester as a wealthy man I was teased and mocked rather than welcomed as a prosperous entrepreneur. So I used my money, a hundred grand it was, to help people at first. I bought up houses and let them at low rents. I provided entertainment and shops in the area. Then, as the city council wanted to knock the houses down and build tower blocks, my bingo hall became a casino. Glen Dalby set up another casino in opposition to me and blamed me for telling the police about his drugs deal when he ended up in jail. Just because I had a Welsh accent. Nobody would believe me that I couldn't have done it.'

'This is just a bleeding heart story. It still doesn't explain why we're here, tied up,' I interrupted.

'You're tied up because you are going for a swim shortly. If I'm feeling generous, you will be shot first. If I'm not, you can drown slowly. So shut up.'

By now, Louise was in tears. She took up the conversation.

'I've only ever worked hard for you. I've brought in new customers and all I get is a beating and now…'. She dissolved into more sobbing unable to complete the sentence. We had been given a sentence of death. Unless I could have an effect on events. I had sensed that the cord around my wrists, hurriedly tied in the dark, might have been easing. Nobody had checked our bonds when we were moved in here. While Curtis had been speaking, he was unaware that I had been working behind my back to untie myself. He was ready to go on.

'We'll deal with you later, lady' he said. 'As I was saying, I didn't do it, but I know who did. Someone else with a Welsh accent. There was a solicitor working for the prosecution, Pearce by name. He didn't know it, but in those days, CCTV was in its infancy, and I knew that he had been in and made that call from my casino. There was also a lot of fighting between gangs, drive-by shootings and such, so it was easy to punish him without anyone finding out who did it.'

'You had Sallie shot?' I exclaimed.

'She'd done nothing to you. Monster! Killer!' Louise was frustrated by her bonds.

'Call me what you like, my dear. I've had worse. But he framed me for that. It was just another incident where I was blamed for something I didn't do.'

'Boo hoo, 'I taunted. 'Nobody loves me. What do you expect? You cheated all those old people out of their homes, you had an innocent lady shot; you pushed a window cleaner off his ladder; you've had Jimmy killed; probably the same for Tilly; Glen's car crash was down to you; you attacked Louise for no reason and to top it all, you're responsible for the deaths of twenty Korean immigrants. So don't expect any sympathy from me.'

Through all that, I could see that he was coming to the boil.

'Don't you lecture me, soldier boy!' he growled.

Now that was a description of me that I hadn't heard for years, not since I fought with Rees Griffin on the roof of Frondeg. My head swam with thoughts of dealing with our current predicament mixed up with thirty-year-old memories.

'I see you're putting two and two together,' he went on. 'Yes, thirty years ago, I was outside Frondeg when it went up in flames, trying to stop cowardly people leaving. Everyone inside died, but I knew where the safe was. When the flames died down, I went in and helped myself. There was nothing to stop me. That's where my fortune came from.'

'So, you got lucky. Why are you still so worried about teasing and ridicule?'

He came from behind the table and stood before me, defiantly.

'This is why, soldier boy!' he said, and pulled his hoodie back and turned his head.

He had only one ear.

Time rolled back to a fight with two men in my cottage. The room was trashed. I had knocked one of the men through the window, the other fell into a display cabinet, broken glass from which sliced off one of his ears. I never knew his name was Curtis Jandrell. He was one of the pair who had killed my faithful Nell.

I reared up from the chair, my hands free at last, and took him by the throat. I pushed him backwards, off balance and taken by surprise, back and back into one of the frameless windows overlooking the canal. In the heat of the moment I found the

228

strength to lift him up and over the window ledge and backwards into the canal.

I turned and ran to Louise, untied her hands and we ran for the door. Obi and Dola met us.

'Your boss,' I pointed towards the canal, 'He's fallen in. Get him out quickly.' They responded as expected, leaving us free to leave. We ran to my car.

'Where are we going?' Louise wanted to know.

'Police. I have an appointment with Natalie Thorpe. I'm sure she'll be glad to see us.'

Forty Five

On the way, I asked how she had managed to text me to come out to her.

'I didn't. Curtis did. I was tied up by then and he took my phone to use me as bait to get you there.'

'How did you get there?' I asked.

'He was being very pleasant this morning. He said he was thinking of buying another property and said he would welcome my opinion. It was only a short walk up to Whapshott Mill. When we got inside, Obi and Dola were there to meet us and they tied me up and gagged me. It was horrible in that room, in the dark. I couldn't warn you when you came in.'

'No problem,' I said, as we pulled into the police yard.

Five minutes later, we sat in Natalie Thorpe's office, coffees in hand, still composing ourselves after the excitement of the morning.

'You're a double-edged sword, Mr Evans,' Natalie said.

'How come?'

'You have given us a lot of work and at the same time you have saved us a lot of work, so, on balance, it's a 'thank you' from Greater Manchester Police. Just to sum up, we have a list as long as your arm of matters to charge Curtis Jandrell and I have a team out arresting him at this very moment. The list includes the murder of Tilly Bolton, incitement to the murder of Jimmy Quayle, money laundering, people smuggling, illegal puppy farm and other ancillary crimes. He'll be going away for a very long time.'

'You might want to let him change his clothes before you bring him in. He went swimming this morning,'

Natalie raised an eyebrow. I continued,

'He wanted us to go in too, but we declined. Didn't fancy the canal at this time of year.'

She smiled, the eyebrow still raised quizzically, not completely understanding my explanation.

'Then there's Gavin Scott. We've traced the gun that did the shooting at the computer shop to him, following ballistic tests, so we arrested him this morning. CCTV on the road outside the Dragon's Lair showed him attaching the bomb to the car, confirmed by the owners of the repair truck that he borrowed, under threat, I may add, to camouflage his activity. He will be facing two murder charges.'

'Darren and Chaz,' I explained to Louise.

I took out my red folder and produced the invoice from Just Computers to Curtis Jandrell.

'This will give you a connection between Curtis and Sperrymoor Farm. In addition, one of his employees, Bella, was involved in the sale of the puppies. She would be worth questioning. The Chuckle Brothers...'

'Who?'

'Two Nigerians. Their name is Chukwa, but you can see how it could be misconstrued. Obi and Dola Chukwa. They're Curtis's hit men. They were, I think, involved in Jimmy Quayle's death and probably Tilly's. You might have an unsolved shooting from twelve years ago, a young lady called Sallie Pearce. Curtis told me that he instigated her killing because he was wrongly blamed for the phone call that put Glen Dalby in jail. It was David Pearce, her husband who made the call - another man with a Welsh accent.

231

You'll recall that I mentioned him in our first discussion. It was Curtis's way of punishing David.'

Natalie stopped writing her notes and put her pen down.

'We seem to have covered a lot of ground here. Is that everything? Any other loose ends? You mentioned a Josh Redfern when you were in earlier.'

'Yes. He's very friendly with Archie Moffatt, the financial adviser. You'll need to check out his racing yard. It's up near Preston. He travels about the country in his horse-box and I'm pretty sure he is part of the network that you mentioned that you thought I was part of when I took a trip to Southampton. He has some buildings which are old but locked up. They could be worth looking at. He also has a young girl, fourteen years old, she said, working for him. She says she is from Croatia, but I have my doubts. I said 'Good morning' to her in Croatian and she didn't respond. People usually tell lies to cover up something. She never goes off the farm and she was worried that I might have been police. You could be looking at modern slavery or prostitution or both.'

'Do your skills never end? Speaking Croatian?'

'Two words I learnt on holiday don't make me a linguist.' I laughed. 'It was just a lucky coincidence. If she had replied I would never have known what she said.'

Our interview was at an end.

'We have so much to work on here and it's all down to you. We're very grateful for your input, Mr Evans. Can I ring you if I have any questions as these cases unravel?'

'Of course. You have my number.'

'I think you're in the wrong job. You should be private investigator not sweeping up after children.'

'Not really. Don't forget, it was the children who started this investigation off, not the professionals.'

'Touché,' she said as we shook hands and parted.

232

Louise and I made our way out to my car as the back doors of a police van opened to reveal Curtis Jandrell in handcuffs, without his hoodie, glowering at us as he entered the station. He moved swiftly towards me as if to attack me, but one of the constables dragged him back.

'This way, sunshine,' he ordered, 'and can I be the first to wish you a happy new ear?'

'You're not the first,' Jandrell growled, wishing he could have worn his hoodie.

'And I won't be the last where you're going. Get a move on.'

I found it difficult to feel sorry for him, facing ridicule from his fellow prisoners for a very long time.

Forty Six

Louise and I sat in her lounge, relaxing over tea and cake. There's nothing like a bit of domestic normality after an exciting day.

'You've been attacked, kidnapped, threatened with drowning, escaped and spent the afternoon in a police station, Not what you're used to, I think.' I said.

'Not at all. I was frightened most of the morning. I was gagged and couldn't warn you when you arrived, then you fell on me when they hit you. Then seeing the mood Curtis was in frightened me more. I was sure we were going to die. It's such a relief to be here now, with no threats. Gavin, Curtis and the Chuckle Brothers are all locked up. Hmmm.' She curled her legs up under her and purred contentedly. 'It's all over.'

'Yes, it is. I'll have to speak to Bethan about coming home. What will you be doing now?

'Going back to work for Glen. He was a brilliant boss, not like Curtis at all, as you've seen, and he'll need me now. It will be a while before he's fully recovered and I'll manage the Rainbow until he does. I'd also like to meet David again. It's been a long time since I saw him. We were such good friends.'

'You'll be more than welcome down at Llanynder,' I said. 'I'm sure he'll be glad to see you again, too.'

Following a couple of texts, I would be meeting Bethan and Jess tomorrow on Shrewsbury station; Louise would be visiting

Glen in hospital, then proceeding to the Golden Rainbow to take charge.

As I packed my bags later at the B&B, I idly wondered where she would be in a year's time. She is a lovely lady, in all ways. To whose star would she choose to hitch her wagon - Glen's or David's?

Only time will tell.

ACKNOWLEDGEMENTS

I am fortunate in having an interested family and friends with a wide experience of the world who can fill in the gaps in my own experience.

Foremost in my acknowledgements must be my wife Rosemary, who puts up with me running ideas past her, listening to my readings and providing input when it's proof-reading time.

Martyn Hubbard, Lew Lewis, Andy Jones and Christine Rimmer have all provided information from their expertise which add authenticity to the story. To them, I will be eternally grateful.

I am also grateful to Louise Sturgess, who allowed me to use her name.

ABOUT THE AUTHOR

 Hilton Jones has had a varied experience of life, having worked as a tax-man and a teacher before running an award-winning canal boat firm. His leisure activities included amateur dramatics and various equine sports as his boys grew up, from pony club to point-to-pointing, polo and even jousting! His pen has rarely been idle; plays, sketches, pantomimes and novels have flowed over the years or, in recent years, appeared on his screen.

OTHER BOOKS BY THE AUTHOR

Scarlet Feather

Hugh Evans in his first adventure against an insurgent group in rural Wales

To Whom It May Concern

A whodunnit set in Cheshire in which DI Nick Price unravels a web of secrets to reveal the killer.

Printed in Great Britain
by Amazon